PAUL BUNYAN

by
DARRYL WIMBERLEY

l'Aleph

Darryl Wimberley

PAUL BUNYAN

Published by l'Aleph – Sweden – www.l-aleph.com

l'Aleph is a Wisehouse Imprint.

ISBN 978-91-7637-017-9

© Wisehouse 2015 – Sweden

www.wisehouse-publishing.com

© Without limiting the rights under copyright reserved above, no part of this publication may be reproduced, stored in or introduced into a retrieval system, or transmitted, in any form or by any means (electronic, mechanical, photographing, recording or otherwise), without the prior written permission of the publisher.

The people, the bookless people, they made Paul and had him alive long before he got into the books for those who read. He grew up in shanties, around the hot stoves of winter, among socks and mittens drying, in the smell of tobacco smoke and the roar of laughter mocking the outside weather.

Carl Sandburg

Acknowledgements

One of my chief pleasures when completing a novel is to thank some of the many people who have contributed to the work. In this case, Jamie Lewis, Cheryl Oakes, and Andrea Anderson at the Forest History Society get special thanks, along with Rob Burg at the Michigan Historical Center, Lori Bessler at the Wisconsin Historical Society, and Scott Daniels at the Oregon Historical Society. Dimples Kellogg, Pippa White, and Richard Cohen get a well-earned thanks as well.

This is a work of fiction drawing from fact as well as fable. Paul Bunyan has been imagined in anonymous folklore, in a libretto by W. H. Auden and in verse by Robert Frost. I certainly used those sources and others to create the characters in this work. Some of the place-names, similarly, derive from tall tales, but also included are camps and mills that actually existed. A logger's work at any location was arduous, tedious, and terrifying in unequal measure. The incidents in this narrative involving Paul and his men or his antagonists are based on anecdotes left by loggers familiar with life in the deep woods. Their experiences, unvarnished, are inspiration aplenty for a man, real or imagined, described by Daniel Hoffman in his book as the last of the frontier demigods.

PROLOGUE

Pacific Northwest, 1920

IT WAS THE DEAD OF WINTER IN AN ANCIENT STAND OF TIMBER. We'd just yarded a log on a skyline from half a mile away, a Douglas fir big as a boxcar sailing through the trees on a thread of twisted cable, when I saw him climbing down from the spar. He'd topped off the spar-tree by daybreak and had just rigged a snatch block for a pull from the other side. Even through a fall of frost I could see the double-bit axe hung through a suspender above the wide ox-hide belt, the handle smacking the climbing spikes on the heels of hobnailed boots as he shinnied down a tree that scraped the clouds.

You hear all sorts of stories about Paul, and some of them are true. He was the best high rigger I've ever seen, and the best axe on the ground. That's a fact. But he was not a thing of beauty and he was old. I don't know what old is for a lumberjack. Thirty years? Forty? He was a lot older than that. I was probably in my mid-twenties when Paul was still a kid growing into his bones. The hair, once a fiery ornament of honey or auburn, was darker now, shot with silver and flakes of snow.

"Paul," I let him know I was nearby. He'd lost a good bit of his hearing, and you do not want to startle a logger with a two-bladed axe.

You risk getting cut comin' and goin'.

Yes, he was big. Huge in fact. We joked that a parliament of owls could nest in his beard and when he sneezed it took the bark off the trees and stirred dust storms in Wyoming. That kind of big. And he was big-hearted, too, though not in the straightforward way you usually use that term. Big inside, is what I'm getting at, I guess. Complicated.

He hadn't replied to my salute, so I figured I'd better speak up.

"PAUL?"

"I heard you."

A surprisingly quiet voice. For a man grown up around the bellows of animals and the curses of men in countless bars and bunkhouses and the explosion of felled trees and shattered ice and dynamite, he had a mild delivery, if not demeanor.

"I've got figures for the cut, you need 'em." I tried to anticipate the purpose of my summons. "Damn near a million board feet already. Camp record."

He smiled. Anything related to logging or timber or woodslore, good news or bad, got a smile. Of course, a smile from Paul Bunyan could signify very different frames of mind.

"I need you to write me a paper."

Well, when I'm not scaling I'm slinging ink, which in a logging camp means keeping track of wages and time cards, as well as producing whatever correspondence is required. I purchase for the commissary, too, everything from corned beef hash to snuff. Paul favors Copenhagen.

"I need you to write me a will," he said, and I felt something clutch in my guts.

I took off my bifocals, suddenly steaming in the bitter cold of the north woods.

"You plannin' on dyin', Paul?"

"Nobody plans it," he replied ambiguously.

I stalled a moment.

"Well, who you leavin' it all to?"

"Timber rights to Ti-Wa-Nah," he gave his wife's name in her native tongue, which was the only pronunciation he would tolerate. The last man called her "Teeny" wound up with a broken jaw on the far side of the moon.

"The rest I reckon you can have. You and the boys."

I nodded. "All right then. Shouldn't be too hard. Any particular reason for doin' it right now?"

He slid his axe from his belt, that double-bit demon twice the length of a normal axe, damn near as long as a cross-saw.

"A will's not just a will, Johnny," he told me. "A man's last will is his testament, too. What a man wants folks to remember about hisself."

Well, if that's what he wanted. No arguing that.

Paul looked up to the sky for a moment, as if listening for the voice of his absent wife, his stillborn child. Failing that, he returned to ordinary time and me.

"I don't mind the jokes," he said. "The tall tales. That's good fun. The horseplay, the bullshit, that's all right for the camp. Gives the men somethin' to do when they're bunked down or at the cook house. Beats drinkin'. But I'd hate to have all the other lost, you know, the nub of it all, on account of exaggeration. I don't want you gildin' the lily, Johnny. You don't need to make me out to be more than I am."

Here I was, standing at the base of a spruce tree rising two hundred feet into the sky, topped off in twenty minutes' time by a man two axe handles wide and twice as many tall, and he's worried about hyperbole.

"I'll do my best," I promised.

"All any man can do."

I saw the broad shoulders shrug under flannel stiff with frozen sweat, and icicles fell like spears from a guy line nearby.

"Where do I start?" he mumbled to himself.

"At the beginning, I guess," I offered. "Or anyways as near to the beginning as you can remember."

"Now that…"

He tugged his beard once good and hard and grunted.

"That might not be as easy as you'd goddamn think."

Chapter One
A Place And Time

I wasn't about to compose a document of any length in the wilderness. I needed to return to my office where I had access to forms and notaries, not to mention paper and pen. And I needed Paul to come with me, which was a sticking point for a man inveterately opposed to civilized society.

It's common nowadays for loggers to return home after the day's work to nearby towns or company-built camps. Not Paul. Paul remained among the trees, this time in a railroad car heated with a potbelly stove. "Better than I'm used to," Paul brushed off offers of other accommodation. It took some persuasion to convince him that a trip down the mountain was mandatory.

"I can't do this without you, Paul," I pleaded. "And I'm sure as hell not going to do it out here."

"I got no place but here."

"You can bunk with me," I told him. "It won't kill you."

He chewed that over a minute. Hemmed and hawed some.

"All right," he said finally. "If there ain't no other way."

We took the speeder twelve miles downhill to reach the Swenson lumber camp, a place more town than country, a complex of homes and buildings nestled beneath a blanket of fresh snow in corporate construction. The complex had just been finished the year before, in 1919. These were modern digs, a far cry from the old stump ranches that occasionally allowed wives to live near their lumberjack husbands. And this was a place built to last, with prefabricated dwellings, a school, and an infirmary. Even a movie theater. It was a community of commerce with rock roads and wood sidewalks and electricity.

Paul and I arrived at the railhead around mid-afternoon. Stumping toward my office I inhaled the pine-sharp aroma of resin that seeped into every board and split log along the way. It was a sylvan location, but not serene. A logging camp is a noisy damn place. There were any manner of tractors and skidders constantly railed in from the woods for redeployment or repair, that racket competing with the trundle of railcars and the tuba of steam-powered trains.

Everything breaks down in the woods—winches and cars and loaders. And people. Passing a maintenance shed, I heard a grease monkey cursing over an arched loader that when repaired would pluck logs like pickup sticks for transfer to a flatbed or truck.

As we passed the commissary, several men I knew and a couple of women emerged to greet me—"Hey, Johnny, when you gonna get a real job?" But no one recognized or even acknowledged the hobnailed legend at my side.

Swenson's camp was home to a couple of hundred families with the attending church services, birthdays, and burials. And school, of course. The kids even have their own baseball team. Course, some of the folks in the towns nearest to us don't want their kids playing ours. "Too rough" is the most-often heard justification.

It's a tight-knit tribe in many ways, but not exactly a town. For one thing, nobody owns anything. Every nail and plank belongs to the Swenson family and their investors. Every rivet is marked for profit and loss, along with every swinging dick on the payroll. We are all part of the Company Store.

"Come on in, Paul."

He ducked under a wide verandah to reach the camp's administrative hub, payroll and post office side by side with the general manager's more expensive accommodation. My small castle lies out back of the post office. We dropped off the porch, crossed a verge of frozen boxwood to reach a tin-roofed box of maybe seven hundred square feet shipped in from Portland on the bed of a railroad car.

Paul had to bend to squeeze inside. It's not much to see, my place. Just four walls and a roof for a bunk and indoor privy, though I do have a porch wrapped around to face west and south. I also have a sink with running water, where I can wash up. A wood stove. There are shelves lining the walls floor to ceiling, filled with ledgers of board feet and profit. I'm famous for taking my work home. The camp shuts down its generator at eight sharp, so I keep a kerosene lantern handy, a feeble wick in the deep forest.

My lantern hangs on a nail beside a rolltop desk situated at a window that looks out to a sloping hill up from the schoolhouse. Douglas fir and spruce rising like phantoms beyond. The landscape green and gray through shifting sheets of fog and snow. The taste of gasoline and sweat permeating.

It's a bachelor's abode. The signs are there to see. Socks airing under an unmade bunk. Long johns stiff as a board on the porch swing. I rolled up the top of my desk to reveal a brace of fountain pens lodged in what is actually a pipe rack.

"I carved that damn thing for you, remember?" Paul smiled.

"Back in the day."

"I'm still using it."

"To stow pens? That's a rig," Paul dug a thumb beneath his suspenders. "But then you always were four parts haywire, Johnny."

"Learned that from you."

I pulled some pulp paper from a drawer and snagged a well of ink. A gaggle of youngsters passed by outside, kids just freed from school in boisterous communion. They were towing a toboggan toward some welcoming incline, the iron runners of the sled leaving tracks in the snow as sharp as scissors through a sleeve of lace. Paul pretended to be busy stoking the heater, but I knew he was watching.

"There'll come a time when people will think this was the way it always was," he mused. "Loggers living in regular houses. Comin' home ever night to a wife and younguns."

"That's progress, ain't it?" I quipped, and I saw my mistake in Bunyan's jaw.

"I don't want people to forget, Johnny. The time and the place. The work. What lumberjacks did before all—"

He cast about.

"Before all this business got started."

"When did you get started?" I dipped my pen.

"Was in Canada. I was fifteen."

Paul smiled with the glow of pleasant recollection.

"You never forget yer first drive."

I could only imagine the scene, a boy still beardless rolling logs and breaking jams with nothing more than a peavey or pike pole, laboring twelve or fourteen hours for a buck and a quarter a day. Rafts of logs stretching for miles. "I'd take my turn at the oars or stretch the sheet that offered some sail along the way."

There were any number of perils. Rapids and wreckage. Flumes were built at intervals to get the logs around the worst hazards which meant that rafts had to be dismantled and then re-built on the far side; this pattern repeated all along the winding Ottawa before joining the St. Lawrence on the way to Quebec City. It was push and pull and break and build and Paul would try his hand with the rest.

A young giant raised on hoecakes and goat's milk in the company of lumberjacks.

"How we doin'?"

The legend now scratching a match to the lantern at my desk as I massaged my cramping hand.

"It's a good start," I answered his question. "But it's not the beginning."

"I 'spose not."

"I'm ready when you are."

He teased the lantern's wick and the blue flame sputtered with a tap of snow on the windowpane.

"Truth is, I have no idea who I am, nor where I come from," Paul said finally.

"But I do know where I was found."

Chapter Two
Origins

"I AM A CHILD OF THE FOREST. MY MOTHER WAS A WHITE pine. My father? A caribou."

With that uncertain provenance, I began Paul Bunyan's testament.

"I was delivered on the tail end of a blizzard," Paul went on. "Near the headwater of the Madawaska."

Source Lake is the mother of the Madawaska River that would play such a prominent role in the boy's early life. A region in Ontario, in highlands ancestral to the Algonquin tribes.

"It was Christmas Eve, 1865. Papa was a trapper."

In fact, Piotir Nikolaievich sold furs to buyers up and down the Ottawa River, what the natives used to call the Kitchissippi.

"But he had a grindstone, too, did Papa, and he was good with horses and cattle, so he'd got seasonal work for years in the logging camps that set up each winter in the region.

Piotir Nikolaievich was an immigrant, a Russian, one of those dark-skinned newcomers not welcomed on Canadian soil with the same zeal as, say, your average German or Scandinavian. According to Paul, Piotir fled Novgorod with a young wife, Elina, sometime in the early 1820s.

"Mama was a woman to reckon with. A Finn, she was, only one generation removed from herding reindeer."

Elina's mother was a witch as well, a woman valued, as were many Finns in Napoleon's fleet, for finding the wind.

"My mother used to say that she found her own wind, and that it brought her and Papa west to a new land and freedom."

There was freedom on the Madawaska. Freedom to live, no question. But also freedom to freeze to death or starve. Luckily for the newlyweds, there was still a healthy trade in furs through the 1820s and '30s, the Hudson's Bay Company at Fort Coulonge paying decent money for pelts of martin and mink and beaver.

But by the middle of the century, the fur trade had dwindled, and as did most trappers of the period Piotir Nikolaievich found other means to supplement his earnings.

"We had some livestock," Paul supplied. "Goats and cattle, mostly. And then there was the seasonal work available at logging camps. Papa got work as a teamster, first, and then a grinder. He could sharpen a damn feather, you wanted him to."

And in fact Piotir was busy at his grindstone in 1865 on the eve of the Savior's birth. On the tail end of a blizzard, as Paul declared, and in the dwell of his rude cabin, the aging trapper was sharpening his tools for a return to the logging camp with whose men he had worked for a half-dozen seasons.

Elina was occupied in another pursuit. She was not looking for sharpened cutlery. She was looking at the age of sixty years for a baby.

"If Sarah could conceive with Abraham, so can you and I

conceive," Elina chastised her husband. "Come ask with me. Come!"

"Elina, do we have to? It made sense when we were younger, but I am old, now. Too old to be a father. And you are barren, woman. We are not meant to have children. It's not our lot."

"Nonsense," she retorted. "Put away your grindstone; it's time."

By that she meant time to pray. To plead. Every year they did this, Paul reported. Every Christmas Eve, after the evening meal and chores, Elina led her husband to a crèche built fresh and placed opposite the fireplace where she offered a pinch of tobacco, a sprig of mistletoe, and a hen's egg to the Virgin in return for—

"A child, Blessed Lady!" Elina implored on her knees beside her dark-skinned husband. "A child to raise in Your ways, with Your Blessing. We ask in *Jeesus'* name..."

She made the Sign.

"Amen."

It was the same prayer every year, offered over a vellum Bible inherited from some distant martyr in her husband's lineage, a plea that Elina had repeated each year of the forty-three years of their marriage. But prayers for miracles are rarely answered, and by the time Elina reached her sixtieth year her husband had come to believe it was close to blasphemy to even ask for such a thing.

"It is not natural," he argued.

But his wife would not hear that complaint.

"It is never wrong to ask for a child."

So on that Christmas Eve of 1865, Elina conducted her ritual as usual, and Piotir assented, as was customary. But then something happened that was very much out of the ordinary.

A shot rang out. It was a musket, not a modern weapon. Piotir recognized the report of black powder somewhere in the forest outside the trapper's cabin. A modest explosion, muffled as though wrapped in cotton, its echo swallowed in the snow-swept wind.

Elina reached for the crèche.

"Did you hear that?"

"A hunter, most likely," Piotir answered.

"On Christmas Eve?"

"I'll go see."

Elina's husband was actually glad to have an excuse to get outside, even in the cold. He was embarrassed. It was painful for him to have lived so long childless and unlike most men of the period Piotir blamed himself. It could not be Elina's fault. She was devout and Finnish. Those people bred like Indians.

He pulled a heavy sweater over his button-up trousers and stepped into coveralls fashioned of beavers' skin. Then came the great coat that Elina made with a hide of caribou and fox fur. The hat a cylinder of sheepskin and wool, the flaps trimmed in muskrat. Boots calf-high, laced with leather, sealed with paraffin and fur-lined.

And finally the weapon. There were bears in these woods, and wolves, not to mention more cowardly predators. And no sane man went out to greet a musket shot without some thought of reply. Piotir crossed himself as he lifted the aging Sharps from its peg of antlers, a .52 caliber rifle with open-ladder sights that was still accurate and, as important, reliable.

Then the aging Russian slung a pouch of cartridges and caps over his shoulder and opened the cabin's single door on its leather hinges. A gust of hoary snow chased across the hard-pan floor.

"Are you going to pray for me, woman?"

"Every day," she answered and closed the portal behind her husband as he stepped outside.

"HALLOOOO."

Piotir first challenged the wilderness from the lee of his his well-logged home.

"HALLOOOO, I SAY."

No answer. Nothing but the wind gone thin through boughs of pine and hemlock.

Piotir debated wasting a round. Decided it was worth it. He shuffled a few yards from his cabin in deep snow and shucked the glove of his shooting hand to break open the Sharps' breech. The linen cartridge was familiar in the pouch at his waist; he slipped that ammunition home and with a cold snap of metal on metal closed the breech. Then to find a cap, secure it on the exposed nipple, and pull back the hammer.

The old buffalo gun exploded like a cannon and snow showered off the boughs of trees all around. The concussion rolling from ridge to ridge in the suddenly still air.

But there was no reply.

What could be more natural for a trapper, then, than to look for tracks? Where there was a musket, after all, there had to be some mortal with legs and feet. Piotir reloaded his weapon. Then figuring the frozen creek flanking his cabin would be least likely for a hunter's approach, he struck out on the gentle incline leading into the bounding walls of pine and hardwood, casting to and fro in an unhurried inspection that within a hundred yards of the cabin was rewarded with the imprint of moccasin-shod feet.

"Papa was sure it was a moccasin," Paul insisted. "An Injun, most likely, judging by the size and weight. For sure it weren't a white man's sole."

The tracks led to a break in a stand of basswood where the likely target lay in the snow. It was a caribou, an aging male with a broken rack of antlers. Wolf bait. But it was clear that wolves were not responsible for culling this animal. Piotir bent to see where the ball entered right behind a shoulder. Was a fresh kill, a breath of vapor rose, still, from nostrils bright with blood.

Here was meat to last for weeks!

"*HALLOOOOOOOOOO*—" Piotir offered once again and again received no reply. He pulled back the hammer of his weapon to approach the animal and for caution's sake was about to administer a *coup de grace* when he saw, tucked near the animal's sprawling haunch, what looked to be a bindle or sack.

If muskets belong to creatures with feet, so must bundles stuffed beside caribou. Piotir leveled the barrel of his cannon on the small wrap as though it were filled with rattlesnakes. That's when he heard a whimper from something inside. There it was again, a small, nagging complaint.

He edged over and with the toe of a wood-soled boot nudged the bag from its warming niche and there, pink in the steam of a dying animal, was a baby.

A boy.

Piotir whirled angrily. Surely this was a trap! A ruse!

"GOD DAMN YOU, SHOW YERSELF!" he challenged and the wind sighed in reply.

I didn't need Paul's help to imagine the reaction of his devout foster mother when Elina turned from a griddle of johnnycakes near the hearth of her snowbound cabin to see her husband lurch through the door with his rifle and what looked like a bag of rags.

Though at first she was simply dumbfounded.

"What in God's name is that?" Elina challenged her husband.

"The answer to your prayers," he answered.

Chapter Three
The Shallow Waters Camp

"I DIDN'T WANDER AROUND MUCH THE FIRST FEW YEARS OF my life." Paul spread his hands to catch the heat off my stove. "Mama kept me on a pretty tight leash."

I could imagine. Not many parents find their ward nestled in the hindquarters of a caribou and for months after his delivery Elina, in particular, must have fretted beyond imagination that the answer to her prayers would be taken away.

"What if he was stolen from a missionary? Or maybe a half-breed's boy? Or took from town?"

Piotir's wife spun one theory after another, each as spurious and more convoluted than the last.

"Well, he's ours now," her husband answered. "And unless some jackanape comes right to my doorpost askin' for him, he's ours to keep."

Elina decided to name the foundling boy Paul, after the apostle who was both Jewish and Roman. For several years following that holy night, Piotir's Finnish wife did not let her foundling son out of sight. And for the first few winters of Paul's life he was effectively fatherless, his foster father being required to return to the Shallow Waters Camp where he tended oxen and horses and sharpened axes and saws.

"Where is Papa?" the young boy used to ask.

"In the trees," his mother would answer. "Now, help me darn these socks."

But Paul was not destined to darn socks forever.

"I was probably not much more than eight or nine years old when Papa took me along to the camp. Not for any pay, of course. None to speak of."

Lumber camps varied in construction and comfort, but in general you'd find a bunkhouse or shanty, a cook house and some sort of barn. The Shallow Waters Camp was about a half mile off the Opeongo, Paul told me. Perhaps two miles from his fosterfather's cabin.

"We took a mule up an old skid row. I can remember riding behind Papa, my hands dug into his belt. 'You can hold onto me now,' Piotir told me. 'But not in camp. Nobody holds hands in a logging camp.'"

Imagine a slow and cold commute through a forest thousands of years old. A spray of snow gusting off branches of spruce and pine and hemlock. The soft report of a mule's hoof on some logger's skid. A deer startled from desperate forage. And then finally to see the camp itself, a wreath of smoke over the cook house. The reboation of oxen answering the refrain of horses and other livestock stalled in the barn. And then to reach a bunkhouse of logs and mud roofed with the boughs of trees.

"I still remember stepping inside that shantyhouse. The smell was the first thing. A musk of men. Longjohns and socks damp or drying on pegs and beams. The savor of wool and flannel."

A lot of fabric, undoubtedly, and in every shade of red you can conjure. Lumberjacks seem to have a universal preference for that color.

"And my eyes burned with the smoke. There was a firepit in the middle. I swear you could have cured a ham."

I asked Paul if he could remember any of the lumberjacks in those first moments. He said he could.

"Some big blond fella naked from the waist up. I remember he looked up from a jar of home brew. Sees Papa. Then he sees me. 'Who's that trailin' you, Piotir?' 'My boy,' Papa already had an answer worked out. 'His parents died in the States from the influenza. He's with me and Elina now.' That was the only explanation Papa ever gave, and no one pried for details."

I wasn't surprised to hear that. Even in modern camps, there remains a stovepiped divide between camaraderie and privacy.

"The feller just looked me up and down," Paul went on. "'Got some big damn bones with that red hair,' he said, and then he offered Papa a sample of his brew. At which point Papa told me to find a seat."

Of course, there is no furniture to speak of in a bunkhouse. In those years, you'd split a log to make a deacon's pew, and sleep in what we used to call muzzleloaders. These were bunks double or triple decked.

At the Shallow Waters Camp lumberjacks used straw for bedding, or either pine boughs. The latrine was ditched outside, but I reminded Paul of the spittoons and milk cans that saw double-duty in many a bunkhouse and he nodded agreement.

"Thunder jugs, we called 'em," Paul recalled.

I was not surprised to learn that Paul and Piotir did not bunk in the shantyhouse. For the first couple of seasons Paul slept beside his papa in the camp's barn.

It wasn't uncommon for teamsters to bunk down beside their animals. Given a choice, most anybody would choose the barn's manger over the lice-infested and foul-smelling shantyhouse.

"I slept in the barn. Come morning, I'd help Papa with the oxen and horses and when those chores were done, I'd hoof over to the cook house."

Eating ranks second only to drinking as the most important thing in a lumberjack's life, but not all camps had a cook house. Sometimes meals would be cooked over the bunkhouse's firepit or stove, or in a lean-to alongside. Of course, the only thing that mattered was the quality of the food.

"I've eaten hog slop in some camps," Paul declared. "Nothing but beans and salted pork. Then again, I've had victuals from a pot under a tree was good as any hotel."

But nothing about a logging camp in those early years was permanent. The early shanty, cook house, and barn were all expendable. As soon as you cleared the timber near to hand, you moved on to some other section, never expecting to spend more than a season or two in any one location.

And even the best of camps were cramped and subject to disease. One man's cough could put down half your crew and hygiene was random.

"We did good for the most part."

Paul answered my question in this regard.

"Course, there's always a Canuck or two that's ripe most of the time."

And the men were as mercurial in their work habits as their hygiene. Lumberjacks would walk for the flimsiest of reasons or slights. "Make her out," an axeman would demand his pay from some bull of the woods, and that foreman knew he'd better have cash handy.

In all these respects, the Shallow Waters Camp was distinguished, a clean operation with a core of quite young men already respected for their strength, skill and steady habits. No skivers in that bunch, or layabouts. These were men unafraid of labor.

Start with the camp cook. Paul was apprenticed early on to Sourdough Sam, that infamous gourmand who claimed to be able to make blueberry pies out of pine cones. But the camp's foreman soon assigned Paul the added duties of bull cook, which has nothing to do with cooks or bulls.

The bull cook tended the livestock and filled the wood box along with any other menial chore demanded. He was inevitably the butt of any joke anybody felt like pulling, and Piotir was as unwilling as he was unable to shield his overgrown and auburn-haired ward from the hijinks of the Shallow Waters lumberjacks.

These were men working from dawn until dark, and as Paul recalled they had little time for a whelp under their feet.

"I remember one February morning it was cold enough to freeze a toad's ass to a lily pad. I'd just mucked out the barn and was looking forward to warming up in the cook house with a plate of Sam's pancakes and some real maple syrup when Papa comes up and tells me to take another team of horses out to Dirty Dan Mulligan."

Turns out Dirty Dan was working a good two miles from the camp, snaking felled logs through a maze of stumps to a landing maybe a mile away on the Opeongo River. What do you need to know about Dan? Well, he was a taciturn fellah, though not without a mild wit. Dirty was probably in his mid-twenties when Paul first met him and already bald as a billiard ball. He generally kept a jar of homebrew handy; he wore a bowler hat, and he never bathed. I mean never. Once Dan got into a pair of longjohns, you might as well sew him up because he was there for the season.

On the morning Paul was dispatched, Dan had backed up a Belgian mare to a nice-sized log ready to be snaked to the landing. Dirty had his horse, halter, and chains in good order, but the tong hook wasn't bit into the log's butt as deeply as he'd like and Dan was concerned that with the mare's first pull it'd jerk loose.

All he needed was some kind of mallet or hammer to tap the hook deeper into the log. A maul or even a beetle would serve that purpose, or Dan could have improvised with an axe head or a railroad spike.

But then here came Paul with a pair of draught horses and the chance for a little fun.

"Boy, secure that team quick as you can. Then run an' tell Dutch I need a left-handed mallet."

Imagine a young boy eager to please slipping and sliding a mile or more into the forest on a row of skids slick with ice to find Dutch Jake pulling his end of a two-man saw on a giant white pine.

There's Jake, a blond, pie-faced Dutchman with hair white as chalk spilling out of his watchcap panting with each stroke across from Tom McCann, a florid and gregarious Scotsman always identifiable by the bright-blue handkerchiefs that he wore in an ascot about his neck.

"'SCUSE ME," Paul had to shout to be heard. "'SCUSE ME, DAN SAID HE NEEDS A LEFT-HANDED MALLET."

It's very hard to get a rhythm on a cross-saw, even on solid ground, and Paul's interruption came at a moment when Dutch and Tom were precariously installed nearly six feet up the trunk of their tree.

Loggers often had to go a yard or more up a tree's bole to begin their cut. On the morning of Paul's intrusion, Tom and Dutch were pulling a cross-saw across a white pine that a dozen men could not circle with their arms from a swaying perch well above the forest's floor. The platform providing their uncertain footing was called a springboard, just a narrow plank of wood jammed into a small notch axed into the tree's trunk. Of course, a springboard is not rigid. It's got spring, hence the name, and so pulling a saw on a springboard is a bit like pounding your pud on a trampoline.

It takes hard work to get a rhythm established on a springboard, and Tom and Dutch had just got their saw singing when along came this young bull-cook to spoil their labor.

"*Say... Get... Dan... What?!*" Tom bellowed between pulls.

"A left-handed mallet," Paul relayed that information proudly, and Dutch Jake nearly fell off his board.

"Christ All-fucking-Mighty!!"

Dutch was prized for his profanity. No one cussed a streak bluer or more creatively than Dutch Jake. In this instance, the logger began his blasphemy in English and continued in Flemish before finishing with a flourish in French, or at least as near to French as a Dutchman can manage.

Once he'd cursed the kid to his satisfaction, Dutch dropped off the springboard and directed Paul up the ridge.

"Red Murphy's bucking logs up that way. Ask him."

So Paul dutifully located the famous Irishman reducing felled timber into logs of manageable lengths. There he stood amidst a pile of boughs and debris, a tangle of hair dark as a rooster's comb spilling from beneath a slouch hat.

"Well, what is it then?" Red snarled.

"Dan says he needs a left-handed mallet and Dutch said to ask you."

"Did he, now? Dutch Jake?"

"Yes, sir. You got one?"

Red pulled a pipe from his coveralls. Mr. Murphy always had a pipe. Sometimes two or three. He favored longer-stemmed varieties, particularly churchwardens, but short-stemmed smokers were easier to manage in the woods. Red never gave a pipe away, but he traded them often, bartering meerschaums and briars for pocket knives or skivvies, anything useful. I once saw Murphy swap a cobcorn pipe for a saddle!

Too bad Paul didn't have something to trade for a left-handed mallet.

Red pointed a clay pipe at Paul as though it were a pistol.

"Tell Dutch I've got just what he's looking for, an' next time he sends the cookee askin', he can shove it up his arse!"

Paul shook his head. "I must have bounced around a half-dozen times before somebody told me there weren't no such thing as a left-handed mallet."

A peal of laughter outside diverted our conversation. Paul paused from his testament for a look-see out my window.

A brace of boys chasing a bobsled down a gentle slope of virgin snow.

"They're having a good time, aren't they?" I remarked and I saw the smile behind his beard.

"I wouldn't know."

🦋

Chapter Four
The Independents and
Swede Sturleson

It took many evenings and about a gallon of ink to get Paul's recollections compiled. I undertook the task initially because Paul asked me to, but that wasn't what kept me going. Partly I was sustained by the growing realization that in the process of recalling Paul's life I was reconstructing my own, and I was astounded how much I had buried or misplaced.

I'm older than Bunyan so there were a few moments when my memories were actually more accurate than his. On the other hand, many anecdotes emerged from the logger's rumination that I must have known at one time or another, but had completely forgotten. Paul rekindled those moments with the force of resurrection.

The work began to take the shape of a memoir, and with that evolution I found myself increasingly curious about Paul himself. Here was a man notoriously laconic for most of his life now introspective in my presence. There was so much I did not know, bends on Paul's trek through time and trees that were entirely new to me. I began to look forward to those revelations, to relish them.

Sometimes we'd share a pipe or a chew to get started, and listening to the aging giant, I tried to imagine what it was like to be a boy and Paul Bunyan. I'd get hints from things he said, little nuggets that would emerge from some casual comment or observation. For instance, in one of our early conversations Paul mentioned that—

"Mama wouldn't let me touch an axe."

He could take care of the animals, Elina told her fast-growing son. He could be a cook, nothing wrong with that. Or follow Piotir to sharpen saws and blades.

"But I will not have my only God-given losing a toe or worse swinging an axe." Elina's dictum was observed at home; Piotir would not cross his wife on distaff turf.

But at the camp's remove, it was inevitable that Paul would rebel. It became clear that Paul welcomed the Shallow Waters logging camp as an escape from an overly protective mother. Even so, this was no childhood refuge. Work in the deep woods was hard, unrelenting, cold, and dangerous. And it clearly exacted a cost.

In my modern cabin I have already seen the laughter of boys stop a giant in midsentence. With that observation and other evidence gained over the years, I am able to identify the signature condition of Paul's boyhood years, the single influence that would drive him all the years of his life.

Paul Bunyan was lonely.

The boy virtually never saw another child. There were no youngsters in the camp aside from Paul, and none within a day's ride of Elina's fortress cabin. I suppose that helps to explain why the young Bunyan kept so many pets and why to this day Paul remains more comfortable with creatures than with people.

Paul was always good with animals, domestic or wild. He never resorted to a whip or stick, not even for the most obdurate horse or ox. By his third season at the Shallow Waters Camp, Paul was sharing Piotir's responsibilities as teamster and he got as much work out of a team as his father ever could.

"But you can only expect so much of your animals," Paul cautioned. "A smart teamster always trains his teams as much about holding a load back as pullin' heavy."

A smart teamster also had to know as much about equipment as animals; Paul learned to use and mend a constantly changing array of harnesses, traces, yokes and hitches. He learned to manage go-devils and sleds and iron-spoked logging wheels that could be ten feet high.

But even though Paul was a natural at the job, he was not content to remain his father's apprentice. Every time the young teamster took a team into the woods, he was paying attention to the loggers at work. By watching Dirty Dan and Red Murphy and their mates, Paul learned how to select a timber for felling. How to notch a tree so that it fell safely. How to buck a felled tree into lengths that would yield the most feet of board.

He also learned how to climb. With nothing but a short axe, a pair of spurs, and a wire rope Paul would dig two hundred feet up some fir or redwood, calling out the general lay of land for the loggers below, the run of a creek, say, or an especially promising vein of timber. Swaying with the wind in that aerie, he found company in nature as well.

"You can gander a lot from a tree," Paul smiled. "I've seen otters jump out of a running creek to tumble in the snow like puppies. I've seen ravens pester coyotes to distraction. But there's nothing'll get yer heart hammerin' like a hunt of wolves in winter. The stalk, the struggle, the kill. The stain of blood after. You're not eager to leave yer perch after one of them encounters."

Sooner or later the boy would return to earth, however, often to find some bird or bunny wounded in a fall of timber. You could find anything from a red fox to a horned owl mending in the camp's barn; Paul cared for them all. But the boy's most famous charge and the stuff of legend was Babe the Blue Ox, and the story of how Paul came to be associated with that force of nature is no short story.

What ultimately bound Babe to Paul was a collision of innocence with evil. Paul himself was as blameless as any newborn in those years. Still is in some respects, I would argue. But Paul's path would cross Swede Sturleson's who was another breed of cat altogether, a man born with a need to dominate and bully that only strengthened with years.

"The Swede," as he was known, came to the valley with the aim of becoming a timber baron and to that end was determined to drive out independent operators all along the Ottawa, following every tributary and creek bordering that river to cajole or extort stumpage contracts from landowners or operators.

Lumbermen who refused to go through The Swede for their contracts could find their logs stolen or their camps razed or burned. Landowners were similarly pressured. One common tactic was to find an owner in financial straits and loan him more money than he could possibly repay. Next thing you knew some bastard in default was signing over his stumpage to Swede Sturleson.

If The Swede couldn't acquire the stumpage himself, he'd go after logs already felled and what he couldn't buy, he'd ruin or steal. Squared timber and round logs were identified by a brand, an axe or mallet used to etch a mark unique to each camp on the butt end of its timber and logs, but The Swede was notorious for raiding sticks off sloughs or ponds, often in open sight of the owners, brand or no brand.

Paul shook his head.

"The first time I saw Swede Sturleson, I'd just thrown down some hay and was headed to the cook house. Then I saw Papa coming out of the shanty with his buffalo gun."

Crosshaul grabbed his axe and joined Paul's father. Then came Dirty Dan and Dutch and the others, a platoon of lumberjacks with pikes and peavies fanning out to meet a contingent of seven visitors, a hard-boned man pale as milk in a bearskin coat and beaverskin hat riding a magnificent roan with three men on mules at either side.

"He was a well-kept man and handsome," Paul recalled. "Educated, too. But he had hands like claws, I remember. And no beard, he was clean shaved. Dark hair going gray. Forty years old, give or take."

Sturleson's riders made their purpose evident with rifles or muzzleloaders laid across their saddles, a mix of Poles and Micks and Danes. Their jackets were patchworks of leather and wool over broadcloth or flannel. Their boots were smooth-soled for stirrups, no hobnails, and when they pulled up they didn't dismount.

"You get my offer, Crosshaul?" The Swede challenged without preamble.

"I got your offer for the tract," Crosshaul replied.

"Well, then?"

"Not interested." Crosshaul spit a chew carefully. "Now, if you want to negotiate a price for sticks or timber, I'd be happy to engage in that conversation."

"I got men of my own to fall and buck," The Swede spit from his own horse and it looked like blood in the snow.

He was a big man in his own right, The Swede, and big-boned the way Scandinavians can be. There were four Scandinavians in the Shallow Waters Camp, but none would make a match to Sturleson. The log baron surveyed the camp from the height of his mount.

"Take me about half an hour to burn this place down."

"You don't wanta do that, Mr. Sturleson. That there would just be an ongoin' nuisance."

That challenge coming from Piotir Nikolaievich. From Paul's papa.

"The fuck are you, old man?"

"I am teamster here."

"That your boy?"

"He is."

"Not settin' a very sensible example."

"Good examples are not always sensible," Paul's papa replied and shifted the barrel of his weapon for effect.

Sturleson smiled.

"Use that thing you'll be dead before you hit the ground."

"Won't help you, you son of a fucking bitch," Dutch snarled and you could see rifles lifting off their saddles, but Crosshaul reined things in.

"Settle down; they ain't nobody shootin' nuthin'. This is just business, right, Swede? Other'n that part about burnin' us out."

The Swede rose high in the stirrups on his high horse and spit again.

"I buy every section up and down this pissant river," he declared. "Sooner or later you will cut these trees. They will be gone. Done. Where will you go then? Hah? You will come to me."

Crosshaul acknowledged that possibility equably.

"But till then, we got trees to fell, Mr. Sturleson. And buyers, too."

"We'll see about that," The Swede drawled.

Sturleson backed his mount out, his men closing on either side to shield his retreat.

"I was only a boy and scared shitless," Paul recalled. "Papa saw. He put a hand on my shoulder. 'Easy, son. He's only a man.'"

But he was a man no one would stand up to. Everyone hated Sturleson, but no single operation was strong enough to oppose him. Sometime after The Swede's challenge to the Shallow Waters Camp, Crosshaul got the idea for a conclave of other independents and family-owned outfits to see if there was some route through a collective petition to the government, or some action through the courts that could rein in The Swede.

Now, Sundays at a logging camp are normally for relaxation. You chew or smoke, mend socks, and sample beans and salt pork. There's always a fiddle or two, and if spirits were high enough, or available, you could see a strapping lumberjack cutting a jig with his bunkmate. All good damn fun, of course. Goes without saying.

But in the wake of the threat delivered to his own operation, Crosshaul sent out riders to logging camps up and down the York River, the Opeongo, and Madawaska inviting anyone interested in uniting a defense against Swede Sturleson's strong arm to rendezvous on a particular Sunday at Jean Lafayette's camp on the York River.

"I went with Papa. It was the first time I had been anywhere other than our camp or cabin, the first time I set foot off our round forty, and Papa let me saddle a horse for myself."

Crosshaul met up with Piotir and his foundling son at the York River. It was a weak winter's sun that morning, cold, and the seat of his saddle was no more than a leatherless frame of oak, but Paul did not complain. He rode with his father and their boss upstream past the familiar landmarks of the Shallow Waters camp and onto lands claimed by tribes of ancient lineage.

The boy stared amazed at the detritus of native settlements long abandoned. He saw his first burial platform, the lofted remains of a long-desiccated corpse materializing from a flurry of snow to startle the young boy along with carvings of half-men or half-beasts implacable to interpretation, this as mist boiled off the cold and somnolent river to sneak beneath the bellies of their mounts and curl around their trousered legs in damp lamentation.

And there was wildlife everywhere.

"I saw a lynx. I saw badgers and eagles. I saw the scat of mountain lions. I saw an elk higher than a horse stripping bark from a sycamore tree."

A half-day's ride took the Shallow Waters delegation to the camp of Jean Lafayette, the boss who would be our host and master of very humble ceremonies. Paul arrived at Jean's camp in the company of his father, Chris and one or two other men from his camp, to find that only a handful of men responded to Crosshaul's invitation. Every logger who was present congregated at the cook house, a motley crew chewing the fat between mugs of home-brew and plugs of tobacco. Finally, talk got down to brass tacks.

What to do about Swede Sturleson?

"We are not looking for a fracas," Jean Lafayette took charge of the meeting. "We do not want a timber war. What we want is to find some manner in which we may protect our barns and logs from being burned or stolen. We do not seek to punish The Swede's business. We are here to protect our own."

Jean Lafayette was small for a logger, but well-respected all around. Jean began his odyssey through the Canadian wilderness as a *coureur des bois*, a runner of the woods, one of those storied entrepreneurs whose forbears followed a wanderlust leading through hostile Iroquois territory on their migration north to the Canadian highlands.

Jean Lafayette kept up the family tradition, trading European goods and sometimes trinkets for beaver pelts and furs that brought good prices from European buyers. He learned to ski and snowshoe and hunt. But he was always an outsider in English society, a Frenchman. An interloper.

Jean resented the English. He resented their claims to empire, to industry, to religion. He revered Joe Mufferaw, a logger known for defending French Canadian loggers exploited or cheated by their English overlords. And Jean loved to recall the day in Montreal when another countryman, the famous Jos Montferrand, knocked out the English champion of Canadian boxing with a single punch.

"My father was there to see," Jean Lafayette recalled the circumstances once again at York River. "There were two English contesting that day. They fight and the winner is declared, and like all English his arrogance exceeds his capacity. He taunts the crowd. 'Does any man here care to challenge the new champion? Does any man have the balls to take me on?' With that invitation, Jos Montferrand climbs into the ring. He is a boy! Only sixteen years old! He steps inside the ropes. BOOM! He puts the English onto the canvas! One punch! And my father was there! *Mon dieu!*"

Crosshaul first met Lafayette in what was then Bytown, later to become Canada's capital city. Chris left the States one spring after a year pulling barges on the Erie Canal and headed north to look for any other kind of work. By winter he was swinging an axe in the Ottawa highlands and by summer he was close to broke, having spent the last of his earnings for a good breast of chicken, a half-loaf of sourdough bread and a stein of beer in a dramshop only a mile or two from the Rideau Canal. That's when Chris Crosshaul first encountered Jean Lafayette.

It was summer, very warm. Cedar shavings were scattered on the dirt floor as a potpourri for an atmosphere spiced with stale beer, spoiling meat, and the sweat of men who seldom bathed. In fact, on that particular day, the establishment was taken over by a gang of unwashed Shiners.

The Shiners were a group of self-appointed Irishmen who regularly drubbed anyone competing for a job who wasn't Gaelic. Crosshaul incited little resentment or even interest among those brawlers, a kid of mongrel lineage barely dry behind the ears in boots, buttoned trousers and a jersey shirt. Jean Lafayette, on the other hand, got instant attention as he tramped into the barrelhouse in buckskins and a fur hat, a bag of black powder horned at his leather belt.

Some import from Dublin about the size of an ale barrel marked the newcomer for his mates.

"Here's another cunt-licker taking an honest man's wages, boys."

You didn't need much of an excuse for a fight, in those days. Jean Lafayette was not inclined to ignore an insult, and Crosshaul despised bullies in any guise. Lafayette handed over his rifle and purse to the toothless fellah pouring steins behind the bar, glancing straight past the barkeep to challenge the Yank nursing his beer on the other side.

"Are you in common with these Irish cowards?"

"Don't think much of their manners."

"*Bon*. Help me here and when we haf finished, I look forward to proper introduction."

It wasn't long before Crosshaul and Jean Lafayette were well acquainted, thrown headlong with most of their possessions into a street mired in mud and horseshit. The two young men took separate paths after that dustup, felling and bucking timber all over southern Canada before finally bossing camps of their own, and in that long span of time their friendship remained constant.

They were a study in contrast, Crosshaul as pale as Jean Lafayette was dark, much softer in his frame and probably a hand and a half taller. The Shallow Waters' boss had a habit of crossing his arms when pulling any load; Crosshaul even swapped wrists pulling a saw, which was painful to witness, and unlike his free-ranging friend he had trouble walking, the result of an injury not connected with Irish hooligans.

Jean Lafayette was shorter and darker than his friend, with a face wind-burned to a prophet's complexion. He had a very high forehead and deeply set eyes. Crosshaul used to say that Jean's eyes were stuck so far in their sockets it took a day to see out.

Kind of far sighted, you might say.

So here they were decades later, two men met in a bar fight facing another and more formidable antagonist.

"We don't do somethin' about Sturleson, and quick, we're gonna be pushed off the highlands," Crosshaul declared, and Jean quickly agreed.

But what to do, exactly? Some of the loggers present suggested finding buyers in the States willing to outbid The Swede for tracts of timber.

"We'll never beat The Swede on that ground," Crosshaul

disagreed. "He's got the banks. He's got the courts. Besides, like Jean said, the point ain't to take Sturleson's business; it's to keep our own."

"How? Ain't a camp in the province can stand up to The Swede's men," one of Jean's men complained.

"Not one camp, no," Jean Lafayette replied. "But what if we looked out for each other?"

Crosshaul sighed. "Look around you, Jean. How many we got here today? A dozen men? Maybe three camps? Four? That ain't enough to bark Sturleson's tree. We need forty camps to keep The Swede off our backs. A hundred men patrolling our spillways and flumes and tracts."

"You cain't get a hundred loggers to fiddle together," Dirty Dan objected. "And where'd we find the time? Or the place?"

It was about that time Paul's father spoke up.

"We can meet during the summer."

"Say again?"

"We cannot meet during the cutting season," Piotir allowed that point. "But there is the summer. And we already have a place where forty camps can easily set up, or even a hundred. In fact, there are close to that many already planning to gather."

"And where's that, Piotir?"

"Madawaska," he answered. "The games."

And every logger present knew exactly what the old man meant.

The recreation to which Piotir referred was known as the

Madawaska River Competition, an event held every other summer on a wide meadow near the confluence of the Madawaska and Ottawa Rivers. It was a combination county fair and contest featuring a head-to-head competition between camps of all kinds from all over Canada and the northern states. Men and beasts journeyed far from home to test themselves against the best woodsmen alive, and each year The Swede stacked his men in every contest seeking to dominate every event.

"The Madawaska!"

Lafayette smiled as he tamped a fresh bowl of tobacco in his pipe.

"During the day, we face The Swede's men over axe and saw, and then with night, while they drink and gamble, we will organize ourselves. The people will see us, all those farmers and trappers bringing their families to the games. And so will Swede Sturleson."

"Makes you sure sure he'll come?" Crosshaul asked.

"He cannot stay away," Piotir answered. "His vanity will not allow it."

Jean Lafayette clapped Paul's father on the shoulder.

"This summer, *oui*. And then for sure that son of a whore will know we are no longer dogs at his feet."

Chapter Five
Work Before Play—
the Ottawa Drive

The prospect of a summer's challenge did not do much to ease the labor to be completed by spring. There was much to be endured before running logs or throwing axes in leisurely competition. But winter did pass, finally, those bitter winds and mantled snow giving way to the coming solstice, and with the peek of dandelions from the greening meadows the Shallow Waters crew had felled its last trees. What remained now was to bring the logs from the deep forest of the highlands to landings on the banks of the Opeongo and Madawaska for a final drive down the Ottawa to the Bronson Mill and payday.

At every turn expecting some sabotage from The Swede.

"We knew Sturleson meant mischief," Paul assured me. "We had every hand on the lookout. Guards at every sluice and rollout, day and night. This on top of the day's work."

And the work was considerable. A single log could weigh five or six thousand pounds, or more, and there were no machine-driven winches in the early years to snake those monsters from the stump to a river or spring-thawed stream. Paul had his teams ready for that task, but those animals could not pull a solitary log, let alone a sled of timber, over broken or uncertain ground. Any snag could snap a harness or break an animal's leg. Without a prepared skid row, horses and oxen were useless.

Paul spent many back-breaking hours pulling stumps and filling quagmires along the rows, and he was cutting skid poles well before he felled a single tree. These were poles cut from scrub not much thicker than a man's arm and maybe fifteen or twenty feet in length that were laid crossways to the path of a logging sled's travel. Where possible, the poles were lubricated, giving the term skid row its literal denotation.

"You hear tales about Sourdough Sam going through enough lard in one season to grease a railway, but it was the men in the woods who accounted for that appetite, Red and Dan and the rest of 'em robbing the cook house to lather their skids."

Water was as commonly used. Some sleep-deprived bull cook would take a water wagon out to the rows on a winter's night and by morning the skids would be glazed in ice.

"The whole point was to get your row as slick as snot on a doorknob," Crosshaul summed up the point of the exercise nicely.

With a team of animals and the simplest of tools, the Shallow Waters camp snaked thousands of sleds and tens of thousands of logs and squared timber along skid rows for deposit along the shoreline of the Madawaska and its tributaries.

You might imagine the season's cut floating as passively as turtles behind an earthen dam, or neatly stacked at a rollway on some river bank, waiting for water-borne delivery to a mill downstream, and in some cases that was possible.

But not generally.

Imagine instead a completely unsorted mountain of timber

tossed on a riverbank at random by some Cyclops, a tangle of logs jutting out like spears at all angles a hundred or two hundred feet high. Sometimes loggers would find the carcass of a buck or doe in that pile, animals fleeing wolves only to find a deathtrap. This was the mess that each year had to be untangled, a pile of sticks slick with spume and ice that had to be sorted one log at a time, or else the work of a winter and spring, not to mention its profit, would be lost.

And time was precious. A rush of headwater does not wait and it does not last forever. Paul and the other drivers had only days, sometimes only hours to sort the season's cut, a single line of men coaxing logs the size of railroad cars from the top of the pile to the bottom with piked poles as slender and insubstantial as wands.

"Busting the pile" was how Dirty Dan described the work and it was treacherous labor. A pile of logs shifts beneath a logger's boots as if alive, and a log could break loose at any moment. Paul learned quickly to distinguish the creak of heavy timber from the "craaack" that signified a runaway. It always happened when least expected, a marauding stick taking one man or the line of men on a reckless plunge to the water below.

But of all the hazards challenging Paul and the other drivers, nothing was more dreaded than a logjam. Once on the Ottawa, the Shallow Waters drivers assembled their branded logs into a massive raft that took its place with the rafts of dozens of other crews sharing the waterway. These rafts were necessary, but also vulnerable to almost any obstruction.

A boulder, a bend, a badly built flume—the cause didn't matter. A single untoward timber could jam the whole river and with tens of thousands of candidates coursing along the swollen currents, bottlenecks were inevitable. Paul was only a day or two away from completing his first drive when the Shallow Waters raft disintegrated in a jam on the Ottawa and blocked timber for miles.

It was a dangerous jam to work, a forest of wood caught in a run of river that was narrow and fast-running with no sandbar or shallows for retreat. Any shift of current could put a man into the water and immediate peril. Imagine yourself slipping off a log of white pine for a plunge into freezing water. You try to fill your lungs with air as an anchor of coveralls, flannels and boots drags you beneath a shifting carpet of bark and wood. You flounder breathless in the icy current, striking out for a log, any log within reach. You find a stick and you try to pull yourself on top, but the bark is seal-slick and the log rolls from under your numbing hands.

In such straits, loggers were crushed like beetles, and even if you dodged that fate and avoided being trapped beneath the sticks, you'd still likely drown. River pigs in caulked boots do not make good swimmers which is one damn good reason to keep a bateau handy.

The bateau is a shallow boat, small and maneuverable, an ideal shell for skirting the perimeter of a logjam or for penetrating its uncertain center. Crosshaul was the walking boss that day and it was he who put Paul into a bateau with Shot Gunderson with orders to scout the jam. Sometimes a single log would do the trick. Pull the key log and you might unravel a sweater of a million threads. On the other hand you might pull a hundred logs to no effect, in which case the crew would be forced to dynamite the constipated timber.

It was no accident that Crosshaul picked Shot Gunderson to

lead the jam crew. Besides being the camp's most experienced driver, Gunderson was arguably the best log-runner in the Algonquins. Chris used to say that a stick in open water was as steady under Shot's boots as a stool under his butt. He was the right man for the job.

But these were sticks as dangerous as dynamite, and there was no telling when or where they might explode. Approaching the blockade, Paul saw logs jammed into piles twenty feet or more over the water, and it was into that morass that Gunderson ordered the fragile bateau, looking for a slender alley of water to penetrate the shifting labyrinth.

Paul worried that their delicate craft would be cut off from any escape.

"Gettin' boxed in here, don't you think, Shot?"

"Just hold 'er steady."

Paul entered a maze of a thousand fickle pathways, a sliver of silver water inviting passage only to disappear as the river's current shifted timber on either side. A bateau caught in that tease would be crushed like an eggshell, and so Paul was very grateful to follow Gunderson's final instruction.

"This'll have to do."

Paul back-paddled cautiously to kill the bateau's momentum and Gunderson stepped out onto a pine log as lightly as a dragonfly lighting on a daisy.

"Wait here."

Shot began working his way to the locus of the jam, using his pike pole to probe at intervals hoping to find a key-log that would break the impasse. Paul's job was to keep the boat handy for Shot's return.

"Here she is, I do believe!" Shot called out, and with his pole and much effort dislodged a thirty foot log.

Nothing happened. Not a goddamned thing.

"Well, shit."

Gunderson turned his back to look farther upstream for another candidate, his first choice apparently a dud, but then there came a sound that Paul would hear many times in his life, a low groan as some animal waking, a voice deep inside the pile complaining, and Paul saw the log pop loose.

"*Shot!*"

Too late. The stick grazed Gunderson at the hip and threw him like a ragdoll into a house of wooden cards, thousands of logs crashing on all sides as the jam broke in a stunning concussion of wood and water.

Loggers ashore screamed prayers and curses, and then watched aghast as Paul leaped from the bateau and scrambled like a crab over hot rocks to reach his partner. Shot was knocked out. Out cold. So here you have a two-hundred-pound man limp as a sack of wet cow shit in the middle of a breaking logjam.

Everyone could see what was happening. Men from other crews saw Paul Bunyan grab Shot's pike pole as he dragged the logger like a gunny sack over rolling timber in a desperate race for a shell-sized boat caught in an angry boil.

"Don't why I grabbed the pike," Paul grunted. "I already had a handful with Gunderson, and he was dead damn weight. And with the logs closing in on the bateau the thought did occur that I was about to be dead weight myself."

Paul shoved Shot into an alley of water and then jumped in after. The bateau was being pulled away, logs milling in the thousands like a chase of bulls. Sucking the flimsy boat along in their wake.

"God, was that water cold. I couldn't breathe. I just kept churning, churning. But then the bateau started pulling away and I saw sticks coming from all around and I thought, well, this is it. But then I felt the pole in my hand."

Paul lunged the pike pole toward the bateau and actually punched a hole just below the gunwale, but that was all right. If he couldn't get to the boat himself, Paul could now make the boat come to him. The kid snagged the hull with his pole and hauled 'er over, but he still had a grown man in wool and boots weighing like a lodestone, and now there were logs barely an arm's length on either side set to crush his thin-hulled salvation like a pecan shell.

Paul managed it. He reached the boat. He hauled Gunderson in and, keeping an anvil of logs at bay with his slender pike, oared the bateau through the merest ribbon to the river beyond. Then the young driver collapsed in a heap until fetched off the water in a longboat sent in rescue from the far shore.

A boy of fifteen saved a grown man's life on that cold, spring day and Shot Gunderson, forever limited by a busted hip, remained faithful to Paul for the rest of his life. As for the other men in the Shallow Waters Camp, and those who witnessed the incident on all sides—?

Well, let's just say that this day is as good as any to mark the time and place where stories about Paul Bunyan began to circulate.

Chapter Six
Pay Day, Brothels, and Hel Helson

"Remember the first time you and me met, Johnny?"

Well, of course, I did. It was at the Bronson Mill, only two days after Paul dragged Shot Gunderson out of that jam on the Ottawa. Shot would have to be transported downstream by wagon. Paul declined that ride, remaining behind with the other drivers to guide their raft of logs on its last stretch to reach the famous mill at Chaudière Falls.

Many mills of that era drove their saws with the weight of falling water. Mr. Bronson's was an enormous and multi-storied marvel constructed atop pilings to straddle a boil of water still known as The Big Kettle. The clash of the drive-wheel combined with the fall's plunge to raise a calamity that defeated any but shouted conversation along with a mist that floated like a cloud, day and night.

It was something to see, and hear, even by the standards of the Gilded Age. An elaborate observation deck brought gentlemen and ladies in top hats and parasols to enjoy the experience. Paul must have been a sight himself, a beardless yokel in shagged britches and nailed boots towering among those sophisticates. Gawking at the collision of industry and nature.

I was employed at the mill as a scaler, a completely anonymous cog among something like three hundred employees. It was my job to calculate with precision the board feet of timber delivered to the mill, and to make sure the sticks were of good quality. Loggers get paid based on pennies per foot, which means that a mill's scaler is always caught between opposing interests. On the one hand, cutting crews want to see as many board feet as possible recorded on the tally sheet, while on the other, mill owners want to pay as little as possible for the delivered deals.

No matter what you do, one party or the other feels like he's cheated.

"I wouldn't trust a scaler with the sweat off my balls," Dirty Dan liked to say when he was sure I could hear.

I don't have a particular memory of how I met Dan or Jean Lafayette or the other men in their camps, but I recall as though it were yesterday the morning I met Paul Bunyan. I was at the log pond, my Doyle ruler in hand, when Crosshaul came limping toward me in the company of some redheaded kid who, if he'd been felled for sawing, would scale out at least six and a half feet.

"So who's payin' you off?" Crosshaul challenged me.

"Same son of a bitch cheats you," I replied and the kid threw back his head and bellowed.

My God, not a whisker on his face and he had a laugh like a foghorn.

"Three hundred and eight thousand board feet," Crosshaul waited for me to dispute his scale.

Turned out Chris actually sold himself short by nearly twelve thousand board feet. The Shallow Waters boss was pleasantly surprised to learn he'd got three hundred and nineteen thousand feet of timber to the mill.

"Thank you, Johnny."

I walked Crosshaul and Paul back to the main office where the other loggers were champing at the bit to be paid. As soon as Chris had cash in hand, he personally cut each man present the share he'd earned.

"Let's find what's waitin', boys!" Red Murphy jammed his pay under his belt. "First round's on me!"

There'd be a hot time in the old town that night.

Of course, Shot Gunderson wasn't going to town, not that night nor anytime soon. And Crosshaul was not about to leave Shot to fend for himself which was not, I should hasten to say, a commitment embraced by most bulls or owners. It would be years before a court case obliged owners to compensate loggers injured on the job and from the reaction to be gleaned from trade publications and editorials you'd have thought the timber industry would surely bleed to death as a result.

It didn't.

"Any idea where we can take him, Johnny?"

"I'll see what I can do," I replied.

I contacted the physician at the Bronson infirmary who agreed to treat Gunderson "on the side". Paul helped Crosshaul cart the injured logger to the mill as I trailed behind.

The infirmary crowded probably a dozen beds into an open

bay that throbbed with the concussion of the mill's fall-driven saw. There were no screens or windows in that space, no curtains or other concessions to privacy. I saw nothing but bedpans for elimination, and every bed was occupied, some men recovering from amputations, others afflicted with malaria or other ailments. Paul wheeled Gunderson to an examining table under the jaundiced eye of the infirmary's sole doctor and surgeon.

"How you doin', Mr. Gunderson?"

"Been better."

He was terrified, of course. The prospect of any surgery in those years put water in your bowels. Doctor Grierson got his experience taking the limbs of Union soldiers in the war. Yankee troops were, for the most part, lucky to have surgeons with reliable means of anaesthesia available; Doc favored chloroform and was practiced and fast. Even so, men died under the knife on a regular basis, and recovery was brutal.

"Let's don't get ahead of ourselves," Grierson offered Shot that slim reassurance.

A pair of nurses stood by, modest Nightingales in long dresses and sleeves, but even the nape of a woman's neck was enough to get Paul hard. Aside from his mother, he'd never seen a woman except at a distance, and you can bet puddles to poodles the nurses had never seen anything like Paul. He must have seemed Brobdingnagian, a boy already six and a half feet tall with a caribou coat over flannels and button-up trousers and boots the size of buckets. A strapping kid full of cum in a room of men spent and sick.

Made for what you might call a change of scenery.

"Put him on the table," the doc ordered, and Paul cradled Shot onto that sterile manger as though he were a bale of hay.

Course, Shot was either screaming or swearing the whole time. The doctor gave Shot enough laudanum to sleep him through summer, and within ten minutes had done everything else he could do. Crosshaul offered compensation in cash.

"He still needs watching," Grierson took the wad peremptorily. "I set the break, but it's going to need some time to knit, an' it can't be here. Infirmary's for employees only. You'll have to take him someplace else."

"I know a woman can put him up," I offered on Crosshaul's behalf. "It's not a boarding house, exactly, but she lets rooms."

"This man's going to need more than a room," Doc warned. "He needs somebody close by day and night. This break gets infected or, God forbid, clots, somebody's gonna have to fetch me and be quick about it."

Paul turned to Crosshaul.

"Boss, I could stay with him."

"Who is this boy again?" I asked Chris.

"The grinder's son," Crosshaul answered. "Piotir's kid."

"He ain't no kid," Shot Gunderson moaned from his cot. "That man saved my life."

That was when I was formally introduced to Paul Bunyan. Except he wasn't known as Bunyan then. Not yet.

He had manners, though. Elina taught him well.

"Name's Paul, sir. Paul Christian Nikolaievich."

We shook hands. Which is to say my hand disappeared inside his.

"Jonathan, but everybody calls me Johnny." I blinked. "Johnny Inkslinger."

"Better than Johnny Scaler, I reckon," the kid replied wryly and I found myself chuckling with everyone else.

"Let's get Shot settled," I suggested. "Then I'll buy you boys a steak."

I borrowed a wagon from the drying yard for Shot's transport. With Crosshaul at the reins, me navigating, and Paul tending Gunderson in the bed behind, we eased along streets ranging from mud to rocks before hitting the more settled avenues in the city that Swede Sturleson claimed as his own.

That ride was an eye-opener for Paul. Ottawa was a place of unsettling contrasts in those years, even for men jaded by wide experience, the gilded and gated mansions of timber barons rising behind wrought-iron gates within a slingshot of open sewers and doorless shanties. Spring irises and day lilies blooming in the flowerboxes of white-washed homes that faced a pauper's grave.

The unwashed still used candles to light their dingy rooms, or whale oil, but the streets of commerce and many of the better homes were lit with gas. At night you could see those lamps wink on, one by one, like emerging stars.

It was a place where thrift and industry alternated with soirees and opulence, a region where the industrial age met whips and buggies, where streetcars competed with carriages for right-of-way. Paul was particularly astonished at that horseless transportation, the cars running off their overhead lines.

"What's in the wire?" the kid asked me, and I told him it was bottled lightning.

"Lightning?!" he exclaimed as though it were magic.

And in fact magic lived alongside science in Ottawa. It was a town filled with ghosts and spirits. Pick up most any penny-paper and you'd see sworn accounts of malignant presences or poltergeists pilfering pillows and sheets in the most respectable hotels. The best homes sponsored séances to attend the cryptic communications of the dead. This was a town steeped in Calvinist rectitude and Presbyterian snobbery, but superstition lurked just beneath that self-assured surface.

The old aristocracy was dying, though you could see their remains in the manors wilting in disrepair behind failing stone walls. The new money was asserting itself, those nouveau riche of a gilded age, which made for some uneasy colloquies. The Dramatic Club, for instance, found patronage with the Earl of Dufferin and anyone who could pay the fee was a member in very good standing. It was rumored that Swede Sturleson had contributed a thousand dollars to the Earl's pet charity, gaining a reputation thereby as a man both cultured and generous.

In fact, The Swede did not give two shits about Shakespeare or the opera, but he was jealous of his reputation and he understood that a patron of these things, as much as fine carriages or top hats, identified a man as having distinction along with means. It was unprofitable to challenge Sturleson's reputation, not to say his honesty or honor. The Swede had a pair of duels to his credit. One man, the son of a banker, died with a musket ball in his lungs. The other well-heeled challenger fled the city, leaving his pride and his purse behind.

The Swede was not civilized by art or philanthropy. Raised Catholic in a Lutheran country, he'd always been an outlier. He was adopted while still in grammar school, raised by a well-off physician married to a Catholic woman who miscarried three times under her husband's care before convincing him that the Lord and Saint Joseph meant for them to express their charity by other means.

Thor Haraldsen became that means, a parentless boy brought into the Sturleson's home after years in a Stockholm orphanage had taught him that bullies, though never loved, usually survived. The Sturlesons gave their name and fortune to Master Thor, sparing neither the rod nor Holy Scripture in his education, this last conducted under the eyes of Jesuits rare among Sweden's parochial class.

Despite these attentions, or perhaps because of them, there were signs of darkness in the boy that went undiagnosed or unnoticed. For example, Thor was probably eleven or twelve when his stepmother began to complain to neighbors that something dreadful was preying on the house cats that were her constant focus of affection.

"The most gruesome injuries!" she shuddered. "There must be a dog gone rabid in the neighborhood."

A long-lived dog, apparently, because for years it was common knowledge that pets of any description met untimely deaths in the Sturleson's otherwise bourgeois home.

Thor Sturleson had a mixed reputation at school, on the one hand noted for vicious tackles on the soccer field and for fistfights with boys older and larger, on the other a youngster capable of enormous concentration with a genuine enthusiasm for history and mathematics. And though he despised Ovid and Moliere, the Sturleson's adopted son became an avid reader of historical fiction. Coming into his teens, The Swede discovered Sir Walter Scott and imagined himself the hero of *Rob Roy* and *Ivanhoe*. As soon as he came of age, he left his adoptive parents and Stockholm, taking a position as a half-deck boy on a whaling ship bound for Novia Scotia.

Swede Sturleson was learning to use a harpoon in the north Atlantic when his parents, traveling abroad, died of cholera. Their adopted son inherited the house in Stockholm, which he promptly sold for three thousand *krona*. With that endowment, The Swede emigrated westward, growing a small investment in an Alberta silver mine to finance other ventures. It wasn't long before he had shares in a coal mine and a few years after that a railroad company. But it was timber that made Swede Sturleson a wealthy man.

For Sturleson, Ottawa was as familiar as a missal, but for Paul Bunyan the place was as alien as any foreign country. Paul had never seen street vendors or the suggestive lures of printed advertisement. He had no notion of celebrity—Lillie Langtree endorsing *Pears Soap*'s promise to keep a woman's skin *young and innocent*. And he'd never seen so many different kinds of people, men and women announcing their status or occupation with choices of fashion and attire that for Paul were as untranslatable as Sanskrit.

I became the kid's docent on our ride through the city, explaining that a moneyed merchant, a lawyer or member of almost any recognized profession would generally get himself up in a frock coat, gray in the summer, typically. Definitely black in winter. Top hats were required for those moneyed classes, expensive headgear fashioned of beavers' pelts was favored, and usually a flowing necktie as well. Low-quarter shoes had come into fashion, probably to distinguish their wearers from the boots and brogans of workingmen, but men of all ranks wore heavy worsted socks.

Ottawa is, after all, a chilly town.

Paul marveled at a family of Negroes huddled near the waterfront. I tried to explain what they'd likely endured. What it meant to be owned by another person.

"Like livestock?"

"Very like."

"And how did they escape?"

"There was a war," I said, but did not elaborate.

It was a society with wealth, but without any sort of security. Hospitals, along with schools and churches, depended on the largesse of barons and the whimsy of those newly rich to survive. Only slightly less dependent were store owners, masons, carpenters, tinkers and oh, yes, the lawyers who bustled like crows on Ottawa's well-lit streets.

Beneath that aspiring bourgeoisie was the working class, those workingwomen, and sometimes men, always living from hand to mouth, these the seamy patrons of bars and brothels far from baronial splendor or winter games, and it was at one such establishment, four stories of wood and shingle about a mile off the river, that I managed to find a room for Shot Gunderson.

Gretta Hertz let the room from her own house and it probably wouldn't hurt to start by saying flat out that Gretta was not a golden-hearted whore. She was at one point an ordinary whore. Then she got to be an ambitious whore. By the time I met Frau Hertz she was an established madam with a half dozen or so girls, but the house had as many boarders as guests, which is an unnecessarily coy way of saying Frau Hertz rented more rooms by the week than by the hour.

Grett, as I called her, survived scarlet fever and hard-fisted pimps to establish a business that scratched the underbelly of Ottawa's newly rich, along with the occasional sailor, lumberjack or deacon. She paid off the constable monthly, which official incidentally got nothing for free on the side.

Grett was successful largely because she vetted her customers. You couldn't just walk in for service at Gretta's house; you had to be sponsored with someone she knew or trusted. The opening qualifier was that you have money in hand. The second condition was that you not make trouble.

Not that Fraulein Grett was defenseless. She had a good height for a woman, probably five and a half feet in stocking feet, with wide hips and dugs hanging like melons in a muslin frock. Her hair looked like a doll's curls, what you could see of it. She wore a beret and sealskin galoshes and she smoked cigarettes rolled from a can of Prince Albert. In fact, Grett was licking a paper for that purpose when I pulled up in my borrowed wagon with Crosshaul and Gunderson and young Paul.

"Well, there you are," she struck a match on a porch post, the fading sun pouring gold down the ribs of her clapboard house like honey over fish scales.

"Where's my money?"

Chris set the wagon's brake as I dropped down to a street of cobblestones.

She took the green from my hand and counted it.

"A little slim, here, Johnny."

"Won't be more than a week or two," I assured her.

"I'll need extra for a girl."

"I don't think Shot can handle a girl right now, Grett."

"I meant to nurse him."

"Oh, no," I declined. "The kid there, he'll do."

"That's a kid?"

"Not according to Shot, but he's only fifteen."

"*Gott in Himmel.* The fuck does he eat?!"

She walked over to the wagon, barely glancing at Gunderson as she took Paul's measure.

"You cherry?"

"No, ma'am, I'm Paul."

"Bein' smart, are you?"

"No, ma'am."

"Well, are you cherry or aren't you?"

"I am Paul, ma'am. Piotir's son."

Gretta turned her attention to Gunderson.

"Does he even know where he is?"

"Nope," Shot roused. "But I do."

She sniffed. "You old dog." Then she nodded to me.

"Get 'em in, Johnny. And clean up. It's time for supper."

"I'm sure Shot could use some victuals," I spoke up. "But I promised the kid and Crosshaul a steak."

She shrugged. "There's a place on North Hinton. Tell Jacob I sent you."

We put Shot Gunderson in Gretta's house, if not in her care, and I insisted Paul and Crosshaul take a scrub. Probably the first time Paul had seen an actual bathtub. Both axemen had a change of clothing in their bindles, but nothing formal. The lumberjack's attire was as unvaried as any banker's. Red shirts, red socks, button-up trousers and suspenders.

But at least the smell was improved.

Took a bit to find the Black Tan Tavern. The Black Tan was an alehouse and eatery on Hinton Street that was built inside what used to be a blacksmith's shop. A roof of tin rested on open beams over rough-planked tables that surrounded the original kiln and bellows. Tools and tongs of the smithy's trade hung at intervals along the walls.

Big Ole felt right at home.

"I like dis place," the hammersmith declared, hefting an anvil for a footstool as easily as normal folks fetch an ottoman.

This was a working man's respite, a roughhewn retreat, river pigs and loggers mixing company with tug captains and stevedores. A tabby cat the size of a pillow sunned on the deck of a wide windowsill, a cheap answer to the infestation of rats common near the river.

Jean Lafayette spotted Crosshaul at the iron-hinged door.

"*Mon ami*! Share our table. Never fear, you may bring the scaler."

I was acquainted with Jean only through transactions at the mill. I knew that the Frenchman had a camp working the highlands in Algonquin country, but at the time I didn't know of his connection with Chris Crosshaul. Of course, over a couple of beers Jean was happy to fill me in. "I met dees man in the company of drunken Irish," he began with that redundancy, and before long we'd polished off a pair of steins for which Monsieur Lafayette insisted he pay.

Lumberjacks are never so generous as when they can afford to be.

"Is it true about Gunderson?" Jean leaned on his elbows in conversation. "A broken hip?"

"Sadly true," Crosshaul confirmed.

"Be a while before he runs the logs again."

"If ever," I amended.

"I heard one of your drivers jumped into a breaking jam for him. Damned fool."

"You can decide for yerself; he's settin' right across your table," Chris nodded to Paul who made a futile effort to become invisible.

"Ah. Is this the grinder's son?"

"Piotir's, yes," Crosshaul confirmed.

Jean poured a beer with perfect aplomb.

"For you, *monsieur*," he offered the mug to Paul. "And with my apologies."

"No apology required. It was pretty damn foolish," Paul replied and drained the pint as though it were water.

"Might want to slow down," I warned the youngster, but Jean just laughed.

"Big man has a big appetite." He chuckled and poured Paul another pint.

It was shaping up to be a pleasant evening. Jean already had a table for himself and three of his men, and I was installed with Chris and Paul at a second table pulled up end-to-end. No chairs, it was benched seating. A swarthy Polack in a butcher's apron was taking our orders for steaks and potatoes when there arrived another contingent of Crosshaul's crew, Dirty Dan and Red Murphy, the Irishman already breaking in a new clay pipe. And finally Tom McCann sashayed off the street sporting his trademark kerchief and a pair of brand-new boots.

Tom's bright-blue ascot was showing signs of wear, and when I say his boots were new, I do not mean they were store-bought. The kerchief may have been newly purchased, but you could bet that the boots on Tom's feet he'd made with his own hands. McCann learned to cobble at his father's side, the elder being a cordwainer emigrated from Aberdeen who went on to own a shoe shop in Long Island. Tom was not meant for shop life, but he never quit making shoewear. As other loggers played cards or plucked a fiddle at the end of their work-day, Tom built or repaired his mates' brogans and boots.

It was invaluable to have a man with that skill at a logging camp where clogs of all kinds took the abuse of saws and axes along with the normal wear of outdoor life, but Tom's craft was a special boon for Paul Bunyan. Paul played hell finding footgear to fit. There just weren't many stores or catalogs stocking inventory for a lumberjack with feet the size of paddles. Tom made the kid two pairs of footwear, a hobnailed monster for woods-work and a pair of fleece-lined moccasins for relaxation. According to some people the moccasins could double for canoes, but in any case, for five dollars and a tin of Copenhangen, Paul got a custom fit and the most comfortable brogues imaginable.

Jean Layfayette raised a beer to toast the Scotsman.

"What kind of fairy is this I see?"

Tom seated himself with a congenial "Fuck you, too, Jean Lafeeeeate."

Everyone laughed. You are perfectly safe insulting a logger so long as you buy his beer, which meant that for the moment Jean Lafayette was immune to any assault.

But just as the platters came out, steaks the size of barrel heads sizzling on mounds of potatoes, another group of drivers and axemen sauntered into the Black Tan who were not so sanguine in company. The cat saw him first, that old tabby rising from the sill, tail twitching. Then Paul nudged Crosshaul and I turned to see Swede Sturleson crowding into the Black Tan with a gang of cohorts.

There he was in that damned bearskin coat, a beam of sunlight winking off the chain of silver dollars banding his pelt hat. His hand rested on the ivory grip of what I took to be a Colt revolver holstered in a belt embossed with brass studs.

"The motherfucker," Dutch Jake declared in prelude to more extended composition.

The Swede swiveled to find the source of that artful insult.

"Well, if it ain't Pie Face." Sturleson grabbed his crotch. "You got somethin' for me?"

"I would get you a beer, *monsieur*," Jean Lafayette interjected genially, "but I hate to waste these gestures."

"No worries, Frenchie, I won't be wastin' any on you."

"This summer, perhaps, you will find an opportunity."

"The games, is it? Heard you got plans."

"Plans? *Si'l vous plait?*"

The Swede opened his mouth in simulation of a smile and I saw a rot of teeth.

Well. Money can't buy everything.

"Putting together a crew of gyppos to meet my men, are you?" Sturleson snarled. "All the pissants put together? Oughta be worth a beer to see."

"You could concede, of course."

"Fuck you, Jean Lafayette."

Sturleson leaned forward on his knees.

"And while we're at it, there's rumors you got more in mind than games."

"I do not traffic in rumors."

"Some kind of mutual defense? All your pitchforks in a pile an' all the pissants throwin' in?"

"Even an ant can bite."

"You're gettin' too big for your britches, Jean Lafayette."

"Or perhaps for yours, *monsieur*."

As Jean and Sturleson fenced, I saw his men clear a table of locals off the one table that lay between our own party and the door. Just swept them off as though they were crumbs, and yet the proprietor made not a squeak to object.

I decided to squeak on my own.

"Evening, Mr. Sturleson."

"Inkslinger."

"Am I right to guess that you're the owner of this establishment?"

"Was. I sold out to some Polack Jew or another."

"I knew there was a taste to this steak," Dutch opined loudly. "Like it was cooked over cowshit."

"And yet you eat it." Sturleson smiled.

I turned to Jean privately.

"'Bout time we found our way along."

"Is a public tavern," Jean's accent improved when provoked. "I leave when I am satisfied, not before."

Sturleson had by this time got himself a stein of beer. He flicked the foam onto the sawdust floor, leaning back on his bench to engage me.

"How much timber you cheat these boys out of, Johnny?"

"Not enough to keep them from drinking with me," I

replied.

Sturleson chuckled.

"I was just over to the mill myself. Seems your boys did all right."

"You didn't get that from me," I came back quickly.

Transactions at the mill were strictly confidential. No logger was supposed to be privy to another's scale. So either The Swede was lying or he had a stooge inside.

My guess was he was lying.

You could see Sturleson sizing up our table, matching man for man. The Swede was a bully, and like most bullies he was looking for an easy target. Someone to bullwhip or beat or humiliate. An example to intimidate Jean and the other independents.

He finally settled on the youngest lad in the hall.

"Say, you. Redhead. You the camp's crumb-boss?"

"I have been," Paul answered unembarrassed.

"Spend a lot of time on your knees, do you?"

"Ignore the prick," Crosshaul counseled.

That's when I saw the spreading smile that on Paul was protean in import.

"You hiring cretins now, as well as kids?" Sturleson taunted, and his men laughed.

"How long you been off your mama's teat, young fella? And how are they, anyway?"

"I bet his daddy knows. Or thinks he does."

This last coming from Hel Helson, one of The Swede's more notorious enforcers. Hel was not yet thirty, nearly as tall as Paul, with hair white as bone plaited in a single tail down his back. Like many loggers, Hel was hard and lean, but there was something inside the man that never cured, some rot deep inside. He was bound to split sooner or later, but till that time came he was a dangerous man.

By now everyone in the tavern could see what was coming. You had two tables of men, one blocking the door and roaring laughter, the other as still as a stagnant pond.

"Not trying to start something here, are you, Mr. Sturleson?" I tried to douse the fire.

"Heaven fucking forbid." Sturleson shrugged his shoulders. "Just a little fun. Fact, I feel sorry for all you so-called independents. Obvious to me you boys is in your last throes. Pretty soon there won't be a stump to shit on up and down the Ottawa that you can hang onto. You'll be selling out to me, soon enough. Me or some other baron."

About that moment Paul turned quietly to Crosshaul.

"Boss, I need to leak."

Chris gave a distracted nod.

"Privy's out back."

Elina's well-mannered son rose from his bench, excusing himself like a kid from a table of grown-ups.

No sooner had Paul left our table than I saw The Swede nod to Helson and as Paul weaved toward the rear of the tavern, I saw Hel quit his bench to follow.

Crosshaul's men and Jean's did not see the threat to Paul; they were occupied with the menace to themselves that was plainly gathering. I expected any moment for the bar to break out in a donnybrook.

"Think I need to bleed my lizard, too," I announced to nobody listening. "Don't eat my T-bone."

Looking back I am still not sure what I thought I was going to do to help Paul. I probably weigh a hundred and forty pounds wet and I've never swung anything heavier than a paperweight. Maybe it was moral authority I hoped to invoke in the boy's defense. In any case, I knew that The Swede had sicced one of his hounds on Piotir's son, and I could not let Paul meet that threat unwarned.

I hurried past a table of drunken locals to find the door that led to the three-holer outside. The privy's door was shut. I saw Sturleson's man take a bead on the shitter, the axe in his hand rising. Here's Hel Helson, a grown man with a stature as impressive as Paul's. That hair swaying side to side in its plaited braid. He hefted the axe like a toy in one hand. Reached for the outhouse door with the other.

"*Paul, look out!*" I shouted, and The Swede's man jerked around to face me.

That's when the john door kicked open from the inside and out comes Paul with the shitter's seat, a long plank of oak thick as a swingletree just ripped off the latrine, and when Helson pivoted to pursue his original chore, Paul broke that board over his head.

"Jesus!"

I staggered back.

There was Sturleson's man face-down on the filthy ground, his scalp opened to the bone.

Paul tossed the board into the swill.

"Did you know he was coming?" I asked.

"He shouldn't of insulted my parents," Paul answered obliquely and headed back inside.

You should have seen the look on The Swede's face when this teenaged kid in dirty boots and patched flannel came walking into the barrelhouse without a mark on his face or fists. The lines around Sturleson's eyes pulled tight. He spit an order to another pair of his men who jerked off their bench for a lope out back.

Paul took a short detour to stand before The Swede.

"My mother is a witch," he informed the timber baron. "My father is a saint."

"The fuck are you?" Sturleson growled.

"I am my parents' son," Paul replied simply. "Piotir Nikolaievich and Elina adopted me, so I will thank you and your men to show them respect."

About that time, one of The Swede's men burst in shouting some Nordic malediction. A few seconds later Hel Helson drags in on the shoulders of his brothers, cold-cocked and bleeding like a stuck pig. By that time the Polack was out from behind the long teak bar with the twin barrels of a shotgun in hand.

"Time to leave, Mr. Sturleson."

"*Nobody tells me!*"

The barkeep pulled back the rabbit ears on his scattergun. *Click-click.*

"You don't own this place no more." The Jew from Warsaw nodded in Hel's general direction. "Time for you to take him."

Some thug at Sturleson's table cursed a challenge. The Swede raised a hand ringed in jewels.

"Not here."

Sturleson swept from the Black Tan with his diminished company, silver dollars clinking above his brow. The tabby hissed at his retreat. I remained with the independents to finish my steak and a pitcher of home brew. By the end of supper, Dutch Jake had revised his opinion to say it was one of the best cuts of meat he'd ever seen.

Everyone laughed except Paul, who honest to God did not get the joke.

Chapter Seven
Summertime &
the Madawaska Fair

Paul lodged with Gretta a little over a week, long enough to make sure Shot was out of the woods before catching a boat upriver on the first leg of a return to the highlands and his parents' pristine cabin. Shot Gunderson remained in Ottawa longer than anticipated, but was well enough by July to join his Shallow Waters crew and other independent loggers for the long-anticipated contest with Swede Sturleson and his hardened minions at the Madawaska Fair.

Piotir brought an ox and a horse to that jubilee, with Paul in company to assist. I made the trip, too. Even the prospect of seeing The Swede's men bested in open competition was enough to make me attend, and I was apparently not the only person so enthused.

It was the largest fair ever. More than a thousand spectators spread over the grounds, some from a hundred miles away, not to mention lumberjacks and teamsters. Paul saw a shoreline thick with tents and bursting with wildflowers of every description, devil's club and black-eyed Susans tramped beneath the feet of vendors hawking everything from rhubarb pie to axe handles. The air was thick with the aroma of pastries and stew and damp pasture. There were always fiddles and fiddle players and Jew's harps and such. Children running about unrestrained. There was even a representative from the Dominion Police in attendance, a fresh recruit in a red jacket and blue trousers as austere as any logger's uniform.

There was music and bratwurst and beer aplenty, but of course the competition between men and animals was the major draw. These events required lumberjacks and teamsters to use their everyday skills in events that were judged for precision, strength or endurance.

A springboard chop tested axeman. The crosscut events tested competitors' skill with a single or two-man saw. Teamsters would yoke or harness their oxen and horses to giant logs to judge the best pull. And everyone looked forward to the birling competition that was the games' traditional closer. Nothing more fun than to see grown men running side by side like hamsters on a rolling log. It would be the first time in years that Shot Gunderson was not entered in that event, and he would not be easily replaced.

Sometimes there were prizes. It was not unheard of to see two men sawing through a giant pine for the incentive of ten Yankee dollars or a gold piece. The animals got no reward, but a winning teamster might get a colt or calf or some piece of equipment. But most of the time the only thing at stake was pride. Every camp claimed to have some champion faller or bucker or birler who was first in the forest, and the sawmill or buyer sponsoring these contests relied on the fierce egos of lumberjacks to fuel those fires.

It was the first time that the independent operators pooled their men to field a united team. The first test of that strategy came with a selection of teamsters for the pulling events. This event pitted ox against ox and horse against horse to see which animal could within a span of three minutes move a thirty-foot log the greatest distance in a continuous pull.

Horses were tested before oxen. A young man from the Twin Peaks Camp would represent the Independents, along with Piotir Nikolaievich. The Swede's teamster, a man name of Brisby, brought a Clydesdale under the name of Ajax to the field. This was a horse standing nineteen hands high at the shoulder. A massive creature. I bet the feather over his hooves weighed twenty damn pounds.

Ajax pulled at fairs and competitions all over Canada and Maine and had never been defeated. The young teamster from Twin Peaks lost to The Swede's entry in the very first round, and Ajax went on from that opening pull to best entries from Alberta to Bangor. He was magnificent. Unbeatable.

But then it rained.

You might have heard the tall tale involving Paul Bunyan and a buckskin harness? Well, it might have been this particular contest that got that yarn started. The story goes that one day Sourdough Sam ran short of kindling at the cook house, and so he sent Paul out to fetch a log or three from the nearest landing. Paul rigged a harness and hitched up an ox for the task.

Now, a harness is not a simple piece of equipment. The shoulders of any draught animal pull side-to-side, which alternates the load dangerously. The breastcollar harness that Paul selected uses a swivel, a swingletree it's often called, to balance out the beast's alternating pull, and the traces hitching the tree to Paul's ox were made of buckskin.

He was barely out of camp with his harnessed ox when it started to rain. By the time Paul got to the rollway, it was pouring buckets, but a little cloudburst was of no concern to Paul Bunyan. Paul just hefted some logs off the pile, choked off his load, and turned for camp at an easy pace.

But the logs didn't move an inch. Y'see, buckskin stretches when its wet, so by the time Paul got back to camp there wasn't a log in sight, just an ox with a half mile of traces stretched out behind like pulled taffy.

"Don't worry, Sourdough," Paul reassured his cook. "It's comin'."

Sure enough, the rain stopped, the sun came out hot as a match and the buckskin on that harness began to shrink. 'Bout a half hour later a stack of logs came snaking up to the cook house.

Just in time for supper.

Now, the grain of truth in that narrative traces to the final pull of the day at the Madawaska Fair. Sturleson's teamster was paired off in the final round against Paul's father. The Swede's driver had taken Ajax through a half dozen rounds without losing a single pull; Piotir reached the finals with the smart, strong Morgan brought to the fair from the Shallow Waters Camp. A coin was tossed. Piotir won and elected to let Ajax make his pull first.

So, The Swede's man hitched up his war horse to an enormous stack of white pine, and when the judges dropped their flag—

"GEE, HORSE! PULL, AJAX!"

Those huge hooves planted like stumps beneath the drive of

a massive haunch, the Clydesdale straining against that load, and as the teamster tapped the animal's flank, you could see that the horse was gaining ground, inching along—

But the log was not moving.

The problem was not the horse; it was the harness. Sturleson's teamster was using the same tack he'd used all day, but the rain had made the traces connecting the load to the harness's swingletree pliable, and under thousands of pounds of tension that tether stretched like a band of rubber. It wasn't twenty seconds into the pull that the harness broke, pieces of metal and hide flying everywhere, and Ajax, released like a bolt from a crossbow, carried the broken remains fifty yards before he could be stopped.

"*Foul!!*" The Swede roared from the verge. "I say, foul! Somebody's tampered with my gear!"

But of course every teamster present knew this was nonsense. The Swede's man did not allow for the rain, and since the log had not moved the minimum required distance of six feet, Ajax was disqualified.

All Piotir had to do to win was get his horse to pull the log six feet. That was the minimum distance allowed for any pull to qualify. One inch past six feet would win the day.

Paul still smiled to recall what happened next.

"I was standin' with Crosshaul and Jean Lafayette as Papa came walking from the blacksmith's tent with his horse's harness slung over his shoulder."

"God damn it!" The Swede swore when he saw what was going on. "Goddamnit, foul!!"

But of course there was no foul here, either. The pulling contest tested teamsters as well as their animals, and Piotir knew that buckskin stretches in the rain so he used the smithy's kiln to dry his own tack stiff as wood.

"SHOW 'EM OLD MAN!" Jean Lafayette and his men shouted encouragement along with the Shallow Waters Camp.

"PULL THAT LOG!"

Finally the harness was set. The judge dropped the flag…

And for a long moment nothing happened.

You could see The Swede exultant.

"HE AIN'T GOT IT! HE AIN'T PULLIN'."

But then Piotir tapped his mare's flank lightly, and as Paul and his crew cheered, the log moved along the track, smoothly, continuously, an inch, a foot, a yard! Farmers, tradesmen and indigents watched that pull with bated breath. Women, children and boys watched. And so did The Swede.

Four feet, five, six—!

The log passed the six-foot mark and Piotir led his horse another six feet down the track, just for good measure. The crowd exploded, a thousand lungs burst into cheers. The woods shook with that tumult. You could have heard those people all the way to the Yukon.

"And that was it," Paul grinned widely. "That was the dinner bell. A twelve-foot pull beat The Swede's best horse, and Papa took home five dollars in prize money."

Sometimes you'd see a man horsewhip his animal after such

a defeat. In a variation on that theme, Swede Sturleson horsewhipped his teamster.

Everyone on that meadow knew that the Independents had a team bent on testing Sturleson's boys head to head, and of course folks love cheering underdogs. But it was the nightly meetings led by Jean Lafayette, the private conclaves of family-owned camps and day-working loggers that tilled the ground for more important contests to come.

It was the first time anyone had made a concerted effort to stand up to any timber baron. The smaller operators could not compete with the big boys for money, but as Jean Lafayette and Crosshaul predicted they could cooperate for mutual self-protection.

"One camp standing watch is easy to defeat," Lafayette told a tent filled with hardened loggers. "But if we take men from each camp and band together, we can patrol our rollways and our camps pretty much around the clock. Will not be so easy for The Swede to burn when we have men with guns looking."

It would be years, decades in some cases, before unions would form to protect loggers from unscrupulous bosses or barons. Still more years would pass before a court approved a suit lodged on behalf of a logger injured on the job, and more years yet before independent operators founded granges and banks, but at least a few of the seeds in that effort were sewn at the Madawaska Fair. The loggers could see this. The ordinary tradesmen and farmers could see it.

The Swede saw it, too.

With the evening's meetings concluded, loggers turned to their favored diversions. Jean and Crosshaul and their team of

Independents broke out fiddles and kegs of beer to toast Piotir for his unexpected upset of Sturleson's invincible Ajax. It was the first win for the Independents in the summer's games, but as Crosshaul warned—"The test goes now from animals to men. And in The Swede's case there ain't much difference."

The Swede was more furious at his early loss to Paul's father than he was at the insurrection brewing among the Independents. A public and present defeat always stings more than a clandestine challenge, and Sturleson had been humiliated before a thousand spectators. His pride was at stake as much as his business which made the coming competitions even more perilous than usual.

Everyone knew how easy it was to spike a man running logs or to let fly an axe in a bucking competition.

"Just be looking," Crosshaul told his men, but even with that caution it's safe to say the Independents slept better than Sturleson or his men.

The morning came with clear skies and a hot summer sun and over the next three days the Independents stood toe to toe with The Swede's handpicked competitors and though they did not always win the axe throw or dominate the spring board, they won enough events and placed closely enough in others to keep the total points between Independents and Sturleson in a dead heat.

Everyone looked forward to the birling contest, more than one logger vowing to upset his rival at the log pond. But there was one new event added for that year's competition that caught the Independents completely unprepared.

Crosshaul and his crew left a breakfast of johnnycakes and sausage the next to the last day of the competition to see a pair of bucked pine poles rising a good hundred feet above a pasture redolent with the smell of campfires and clover. You could see a cow bell rigged at the top of each spar.

"The hell is that?" Red Murphy grumbled as he scratched his balls.

Jean Lafayette spoke up. "It's for climbing, clearly. But I do not see that event on the list."

"'Parently, you didn't pay much attention to 'Miscellaneous'," came a voice from behind, and there was Swede Sturleson, legs spread wide like he was pissing and with a shit-eating grin to boot.

Now, miscellaneous contests were generally events catering to children, chasing a greased calf, or splitting kindling with a hatchet. Not to say loggers in the old days didn't climb trees. Of course, they did. You didn't need a lot of gear to mount a tree trunk.

A climber looped a wire-rope around the tree at its very base, making sure to secure that tether to the belt at his waist. You used your arms to hop the rope up the tree's smooth bole, driving the spikes on your boots into the wood for traction on the ascent. In competition, climbers were required to ring a bell mounted topside; first man down to the ground won the climb, and coming down was actually more dangerous than climbing up. More like a controlled fall than a measured descent.

Some competitors wore heavy gloves; a run up a tree can make for a nasty burn of knuckles. Other contestants customized their climbing spurs, some fabricated to be longer than others, others differently shaped and secured. The Swede's men had their own gear, but no one among the independents brought equipment for a competitive climb.

"What are we to do?" Crosshaul conferred with his men. "We're tied for points. But by the rules if we forfeit any event, we lose!"

"We can't climb barefoot," Dirty Dan wiped sweat off his hairless skull.

"I cud make da geer," Big Ole offered.

"So at least we can enter a man. That's better than nothing. But who can climb?"

Red Murphy tapped his pipe on his boot. "I've seen Paul climb."

"No, no," Piotir objected. "He's not yet sixteen."

"He can shinny like a got-damn squirrel."

"He is too young. These are men. And The Swede's men too."

Paul cleared his throat politely.

"I'd like to try it, Papa."

"No." Piotir shook his head, which seemed to end the notion.

But then Shot Gunderson spoke up.

"Thought we were agreed that Paul's his own man."

You could see Piotir's jaw set.

"He is still my son."

"He's a man, same as us, Piotir. He oughta be able to make up his own mind."

Paul laid a hand large as a plate on the old man's shoulder.

"I don't have to win, Papa. I just have to enter."

Piotir spit a wad of tobacco clear to the river. You could see a war raging in his mind, his heart.

"Something happen to you, Mama will kill me."

"I could have died in the logjam, Papa. Or wound up hurt like Shot. There ain't no way to avoid takin' risks in timber unless I leave the woods altogether which I am not gonna do."

"Well spoken," Jean Lafayette interposed. "And Paul is right. We just need a man to enter. We can lose the climb if we run the logs well enough, but we cannot win with a forfeit."

That settled it. Big Ole loped back to his anvil and tongs to fashion a pair of spikes to strap onto Paul's oar-sized boots. Crosshaul and Jean got to work on a waist-harness. Swede Sturleson affected a smile as he watched the redheaded kid who'd bushwacked his henchman stroll up to the climbing poles carrying a rope of leather and haywire, and hand-rigged climbing boots.

There were two poles planted vertically to test the climbers. Both poles rose a hundred feet above the meadow and both were debarked which meant that both poles were slicker than goose shit. Paul took a position indicated by one of the officials present, leaving the other pole for, wouldn't you know—? Hel Helson.

Helson spit a wad of snuff in Paul's direction, which he serenely ignored.

The judges were ready to start the race but were delayed when Sturleson demanded to examine all of Paul's equipment.

As if that haywired rig conferred some sort of advantage. The Swede had his own bull take possession of Paul's gear and when Crosshaul objected The Swede jerked a finger toward Helson.

"You're welcome to check my man."

Crosshaul spit. "A spike is a spike, Sturleson. A rope is a rope. Give my man back his gear."

The silver dollars on the timber baron's derby caught the bright afternoon sun as The Swede accepted the gear from his own man. The Swede shoved Paul his spikes and harness with a warning.

"It's wrong to send a boy to do a man's job."

"Yes, sir."

Paul took his tools politely.

"Which is why they sent me."

Finally, the two lumberjacks were set to climb. Each man had his rope looped about his respective pole. One hundred feet of white pine four feet through and smooth as a spanked baby's fanny. Helson tucked his ponytail under his shirt before snugging his wire rope above his head. Paul appeared relaxed in the hold of his harness.

A cowbell served as start gun and with that clamor Hel and Paul took off. It was an amazing sight, two athletes digging spikes and slapping rope in what seemed a vertical race to the sky. Pieces of bark chewed from the poles by their climbing boots fell to earth like hickory shells from the teeth of squirrels. At the halfway point they were dead even.

But then Paul's rope slipped.

"JESUS!" his papa exclaimed as Paul appeared set for a tumble.

By the time Paul recovered he'd given up ten feet to Hel Helson.

But Helson was laboring. He was a strong man with endurance any runner would covet, but sixty feet up that tree his legs burned and his lungs ached and his heart hammered like iron on an anvil.

And here came the kid. Paul did not panic. He settled into a swift, sure ascent, the rope and spikes perfectly coordinated. Paul caught Hel at the very top, and the twin bells clanged as though by a single hand.

Then came the dangerous part, the descent, and this was where Hel had an advantage. This was where experience and confidence could not be defeated by raw talent. Within seconds The Swede's man was skipping down the pine like a stone over water as Paul struggled to keep pace.

That's when his wire-rope popped off its belt. Paul was maybe thirty feet from the earth and as high as a three-storey building when I saw the wire rope snap from his climbing belt, the vital tether snapping free with the crack of a bullwhip. A thread of leather abruptly unmoored.

For the smallest of moments Paul seemed suspended in air, reaching for the pole on instinct, as any man would, trying to embrace that awful pillar. Scratching on instinct for a fingernail's purchase on that limbless bole.

And then he fell.

Piotir's scream gargled in his mouth as he saw his only child plummet to earth. Paul slammed into that summer pasture like a bag of rags. Helson touched down moments later and, as everyone else rushed to aid the fallen young man, Hel slipped his rope, shucked his climbing spurs, and strolled away.

. . . .

There was blood curling from the boy's mouth when we got to him, for he was a boy, now, just a boy. A young stalwart fallen in an awful accident.

Or was it an accident?

That question came secondarily. The only thing that mattered in the moment was Paul.

Was he injured? Killed?!

Piotir could not help his son, and this was not Ottawa; there was no infirmary. But God or something like a God must have been looking over Paul that day.

"Excuse me."

A firm, cultured voice cut through the cacophony of shouts and curses as calmly as a spoon through custard.

We all looked up to see a man in a banker's coat but with a kind of wide-brimmed hat and riding boots.

"I am a physician," he said. "John Murphy. May I assist?"

So we had a sawbones on hand, a brilliant one as it turned out, and a man familiar with loggers, too, born in a shack in Wisconsin.

"Don't move him" was the doctor's first order. "Bring a tent. I'll treat him right here."

"Let him live…"

You could hear Piotir praying.

"Let him walk!!"

The doctor at first did not even move Paul off the ground. He took a knee beside Paul calmly, thoughtfully, as though examining a painting. Paul did not lose consciousness entirely, though he was clearly stunned and in great pain.

"What is your name, son?"

"…Paul."

"I am Doctor Murphy. You've taken a spill."

I saw the doc take a fountain pen from his coat.

"Take off his boots and socks."

We scrambled to comply. And then the physician cradled an ankle and raked the pen up the insole of Paul's foot and I saw the toes arch in reply.

"What does that mean?!"

Piotir called out frantically.

"What does it mean?!!"

"It means the spine is not broken," Murphy replied calmly. "But there's a likelihood of internal injuries. I have a bag in my wagon, if you can send someone. And I'll need water, too, lots of it, brought to a boil for at least fifteen minutes. That's very important. And scald whatever pots you use with boiling water as well.

"We must keep the theater as clean as we can. And you'll need a stove rigged or some heat. We're lucky it's summer, but even so I want a warm tent. Can you manage that?"

"Yes, sir." Crosshaul volunteered and we all got to work.

Then we saw The Swede.

Sturleson was standing at the periphery of our misery, as grim as any reaper. Hel stood beside him.

"What do you want?" Jean Lafayette challenged.

"Why, a congratulations, of course. My man won."

"Time like this? You got some goddamned gall!" I would have shot the son of a bitch then and there, I think, if I'd had a gun.

Sturleson shrugged.

"Rules are rules."

"Yes, they are."

This was a new voice intruding, you could tell by the accent. Some local, unschooled voice, and when we turned, we saw it was one of the fair's appointed judges.

He was clearly a local man, dressed out of character to be formal, I suppose, in some sort of cross between a lederhosen and overalls. A top hat in very frayed beaver. He looked like a leprechaun but what he did next made him a mensch.

"Rules are rules, Mr. Sturleson," the judge repeated. "And the rules say first man who rings the bell and comes to ground first wins."

The little man pointed to Paul.

"He rang the bell. And he beat your man to the ground."

It wasn't the ruling that we cared about. I can honestly say that. No one among the independents gave a shit whether the contest was won or lost. We had a man down and hurt. A man we cared about. A young man already loved among men.

But here was a stranger to us, some yokel picked to run a fair, and he was standing up to a timber baron and bully. He was standing his ground against Swede Sturleson.

"Who the fuck are you?" The Swede snarled.

"I am the official charged to judge this event," the local man tipped his hat formally. "And I say this man here beat your man to the ground."

Hel Helson took a step forward.

"You little shit."

"Back off," I heard someone say, and as I looked up I saw some logger I'd never seen step from a growing crowd of spectators and axemen. Then another man stepped forward. And another. Within moments a phalanx of axes faced The Swede and his hell-bent men.

Women pulling their children away, by this time. Leaving the meadow as their husbands and fathers formed a cordon formed around Sturleson and his men.

I saw Helson hesitate.

"Boss?"

Sturleson looked around.

"You think this means anything? You fucking cunts? You think this will buy you lard next winter? Or pork? Who do you think's going to pay your wages come winter?"

"The trees are going anyway," I declared. "You can kid yourself Sturleson, but you know as well as I do your days are as numbered as theirs."

"The fuck does an inkslinger know about timber?"

"I know once a tree's cut, it's gone," I said. "And when the trees go, so will you."

"We'll see about that," Sturleson snarled. "We'll just goddamn see."

"A moment, please."

Once again the calm voice of the doctor stilled the hundreds gathered.

Dr. John Benjamin Murphy emerged from the tent with Paul's harness in his hands.

"Is there a constable available?"

"Got the Dominion Police," the local official replied. "If need be."

"There may be a need."

A murmur rose among those gathered.

"I have no experience with logging equipment," Dr. Murphy qualified his remarks. "However, I do have a great deal of experience with scalpels and blades, and if you look here—"

Murphy indicated a seam between a pair of popped rivets on Paul's harness.

"I think you will see that this equipment did not break on its own."

"What d'you mean, Doctor?" Crosshaul pressed forward.

"What are you saying?"

"I am saying that I will defer to the judgment of men more experienced in these particulars," the doctor replied carefully. "But in my opinion, this harness was cut along this line right here…"

The physician held the harness so Crosshaul could see.

"… Just here on the eyelets, where the rivets were pressed. Which would of course explain why that joining broke loose."

At first the formality of the doctor's diagnosis softened its import. But I realized what the doctor was saying, and so did Crosshaul. And that verdict began to spread.

"What'd he say?"

You could hear men on the outskirts of the conversation straining to hear.

"Something about the harness?"

"Move out," Sturleson muttered to Helson. "Move and keep moving."

And a good damn thing he did, too.

There was a press of men toward the tent, Crosshaul and his men practically fighting to see the sabotaged harness that plunged Piotir's son to the brink of death.

"You son of a bitch!!"

I heard Piotir scream.

"I kill you! I kill you, Sturleson!!"

It looked like we had a riot coming. And we would have, too, I am convinced of it. Blood would have been spilled that night with women and children in the way but for the single, sane voice of Dr. John Murphy.

"Gentlemen... *Gentlemen.*"

Some voices are made to command. The growing clamor rumbled, then stilled. Dr. Murphy handed the harness to Crosshaul.

"Decide now what matters. Do you mean to bring more men to my care this evening, innocents and scoundrels alike? Or would your time be better spent helping me to save this boy?"

Well, that did it. That was the shooting match. The Swede was forgotten, but not before The Law paid him a visit.

It was early afternoon when Sergeant Jack Jackson presented himself at Sturleson's tent. Blue trousers and red jacket. A Sam Browne belt and sidearm. Shaved clean as a whistle.

"I've come to discuss the incident this morning, sir. The young climber. There are indications you may have been involved in a sabotage of his equipment."

"Do you know who the fuck I am?!" Sturleson growled.

"I do, Mr. Sturleson," Sergeant Jackson rested a hand casually on the grip of his revolver. "Which is why I am telling you as a courtesy that I intend to recommend a warrant for your man's arrest, if not your own."

"Arrest. On what charge?"

"Aggravated assault."

"It was an accident."

"For a judge to decide."

"I'll see the judge before you do."

"Then the sooner you leave, the better."

"The fuck does that mean?"

"Look about, Mr. Sturleson. There are a thousand people here who believe you cut that boy's harness. I cannot be responsible for your safety."

"I can look out for myself."

"It's not your welfare alone for which I'm responsible, sir. You will vacate this vicinity by nightfall, Mr. Sturleson. That is not a suggestion."

It was the first time an ordinary lawman stood up to The Swede face to face, and before the sun was set Sturleson was gone, packed up with his score of men and disappeared.

But Dr. Murphy did not leave, nor did a single lumberjack among the independents.

I remained with Piotir.

"His mother will never forgive me."

"Hush," I told him. "Wait and see."

Morning came finally, a weakly breaking dawn. A heavy dew painted the tops of the wild flowers on the meadow with a silver patina. Kettles boiled at campfires fresh with kindling and the women tending those rough hearths brought baskets of pancakes and bacon to those of us convened around the surgeon's tent, along with endless cups of tea.

We waited. And waited. The tent's guys had long gone slack by the time Doctor Murphy emerged, the white sleeves of his shirt rolled up past his elbows. That long face and beard. He had a remarkable countenance, a warm face, but disciplined, too. And reserved. Like President Lincoln had been.

"It's going to be a long road," the doctor announced quietly. "The young man has serious injuries. But he is young. He is unusually strong. I believe he will live."

There was no hurrah raised in response to that news, no exclamation of triumph or joy. Some men dropped their heads. Piotir dropped to his knees. The women were wonderful, I have to say. Giving us food for our souls as well as our stomachs. A pat on the shoulder here. A cluck of sympathy there. Warm cups of tea pressed into every hand.

Bless every woman in Canada is all I can say. I never saw anything like it. And the same for Doc Murphy.

But all the youth, strength, kindness and skill in the world were not enough by themselves to pull Paul through that awful time. He had multiple injuries, broken ribs which were terrible; every sneeze was excruciating. He had fallen more or less sideways and had a femur and forearm broken. A shoulder dislocated. Doc gave Paul laudanum before setting the shoulder back into its false socket, but still he screamed. Crosshaul had to coax Piotir far across the camp before that task could be attempted and still Piotir heard his boy's agony.

The fair folded in the wake of The Swede's treachery. There would be no log rolling or end-of-the-week festivities. There would also be no arrest. No one had any illusions about the pursuit of justice in Ottawa. But even as the fair ended, people did what they could, families and individuals leaving gifts of food or flowers on their way back to their farms or small towns.

An old woman, frail and arthritic, brought Piotir a fresh basket of colt's foot that she'd gathered herself.

"For a tea," she urged the disconsolate grinder. "To help him breathe."

Doctor Murphy remained at Paul's side all night and another day to make sure the kid's gut and lungs were intact, but then he had to go. The doctor had patients waiting back home, after all, not to mention a wife and family. But before the doc packed up, he sat Piotir down with Crosshaul and me and, after some medically related remarks, gave us the advice essential to restore Paul's health.

"This assault was purposeful and malignant, which will complicate the boy's recovery," the doctor told us on the day he left. "The injuries that are obvious will heal first. But the boy's mind and soul are bruised as well, make no mistake about it. I have seen this many times, in soldiers, even, and this boy I'm sure is more innocent than most."

"So what do we do, Doctor?" Piotir asked. "What do I tell my son?"

"You cannot tell him anything. But you can listen."

"What does he need most, then? At least give me that."

"He needs a reason to live."

A reason to live. Would seem second nature for a young giant and yet for many months…

Paul could not find it.

CHAPTER EIGHT
A BABE IS BORN

THE ONLY REASON ELINA DIDN'T STRANGLE HER HUSBAND at the return of her badly injured son was that she needed Piotir's help to nurse Paul back to health.

"Eat." She would coax a fine beef stew into the teenager's spoon. "Take something, Paul."

He'd sip goat's milk sometimes. And sometimes take a wedge of cheese. Sometimes a gnaw of home-baked bread. But that was about all. The young Bunyan did not speak unless spoken to. He did not pick up his papa's fiddle or mouth harp. There was no laughter in the cabin. Paul's sixteenth birthday came and went without remark or celebration. It was as though he'd aged into a very old man overnight.

"Restore him to me, Father," Elina prayed fervently.

Elina did not need a surgeon to know that a deep cloud had fallen over Paul's heart, his soul. Summer passed and then fall, but Paul did not return to the woods. In fact, he rarely left the cabin and when the mercury made the dip to winter and blizzards buried the north woods in drifts of snow, Piotir and Elina realized they had an invalid on their hands.

"What will he do when we are gone?" Elina worried.

"The doctor warned me," Piotir said. "He warned me."

For days and days during winter blows the family would be housebound, the drifts outside rising to the eaves of their well-logged cabin. It was what we used to call a blue winter. The snow would fall so thickly you couldn't see your hand in front of your face, but by morning there'd be not a cloud in the sky and when the sun came up it seemed like the snow took on an icy blue color. Crystals bright and blue stirring in the breeze like spirits at play. That's when you knew it was really cold.

About the only place warm besides the cabin was the barn and that was where Paul sometimes retreated, though he'd never remain if Piotir or Elina wandered in. The young logger would complete his chores dutifully, if mechanically, and then install himself between the horses and oxen where for hours he would sleep or sometimes whittle.

"He is not the same boy," Elina said over and over and of course she was right.

Christmas came and went, and the weather turned more bitterly cold. The wilder animals had foraged all they could. Birds were long gone, and caribou and elk and moose were stripping bark from trees to survive as wolves culled the weak or starving. Life in the winter-wild was hard. New life would have to wait for spring.

Domesticated animals bear life year-round, though, and one of Piotir's oxen let him know that she was about to calve. An ox, by the way, is not a species of animal; an ox is simply a bovine trained for heavy work. Female oxen are not nearly as common as males. Piotir had a breeding bull and three oxen, including a cow who'd got her bag and by February was ready to deliver.

Her time came, she broke, but the calf was breached. This is something every rancher and dairyman dreads because if a calf gets turned around in its mother and cannot be delivered, the mama dies along with her offspring.

"Paul," Piotir roused his son late one night. "Get up, son. I need your help in the barn."

Paul followed his papa to find the ox on her feet, her head pulled between iron bars at a calving stand rigged inside a stall. Paul had pulled calves before. He knew the purpose for the block and tackle in the stall, with its yards of hemp. In the summer this was the rig you'd use to pull a line tight. You could pull a thousand pounds of log with a block and tackle, but that night the gear was meant to be used on a calf dying inside its mother.

"We don't have much time." Piotir secured a noose and one end of the line.

"She may kick," Piotir warned and taking the noose in his hand thrust it up the mama's birth canal.

The ox bellowed and bucked in her iron stall. Paul tried to calm her with words, feeble words.

"I've got the calf," Piotir grunted. "Got the legs looped in pretty tight, I think."

Piotir by now up to his forearm inside the mother animal. She bellowing and bucking.

"There. Got it."

The old teamster pulled his hand from the canal, slimy from fingertips to elbow in blood and fluid.

"Are we anchored, son?"

"Yes, Papa."

"Time to pull."

Paul had stretched a quarter-mile of cable tight as Dick's hat band with a block and tackle, but it took nearly an hour with that same gear to coax a forty-pound calf free of its mama.

The ox bellowing fury and pain the whole time.

The calf came out feet first, a miserable bag of bones and blood.

"What is it, Papa?!" Paul scrambled to see.

"He's male."

The calf was not moving. He was not breathing.

"Papa?"

"Give him a minute."

But Paul could not wait. He dropped to his knees clearing mucus from the calf's mouth and nostrils, and began rubbing the newborn up and down, up and down.

"Paul—?" Piotir started to chide his son, but then stopped.

Here was a boy who'd turn away a spoon of stew now cradling the stillborn calf in his arms. Something in the plight of this newborn innocent had touched a chord nearly dead in his son, and Piotir realized in that moment that if Paul was to live, so must this breached calf.

"Here, let me."

Piotir dropped to his knees beside his son.

"I have a hold. You slap him hard. Hard on the ass, son. As hard as you can."

"I ... I can't."

"He doesn't breathe, he dies, son. Slap him."

Paul reached back and smacked a haunch.

"That won't do. He needs a shock, Paul."

Paul reached over again.

"Sorry, babe," he said and walloped that calf right on a bony hip.

Paul smacked that calf, and it bellowed to beat the band. Loudest damn calf I ever heard, Paul would tell the boys in later years.

"Raised the rafters, he did. I bet you could of heard that calf till next Wednesday."

"A breached calf in a blue winter," Papa smiled as the newborn found his mama's udder.

"We'll call him Babe," Paul declared. "Babe the Blue Ox."

From that moment Paul began to heal in the ways that are really important, the ways that last. The calf needed care those first few days, and Paul was there to give it. He made a bunk in the barn to sleep.

"He'll freeze!" Elina protested.

"He'll freeze if he doesn't," her husband replied.

Winter gave way to spring, and Paul began to enjoy what in many ways was his first childhood. He had a playmate in Babe, if a very large one. Babe was the fastest-growing bovine Piotir had ever seen, and in the months following the ox's birth Paul himself found a new spurt of growth.

They made some pair, boy and bull. Through the spring, Paul led Babe like a puppy for long, leisurely forays into the forest. Unlike Piotir, Paul was not an avid hunter, though he did enjoy fishing, whether by net or line. Within a couple of summers it was common to see Paul straddling Babe's neck like some kind of mahout with the catch of the day hanging from one of Babe's spreading horns. It was on one of these expeditions with Babe that Paul made his first serious encounter with an Algonquin tribe.

Tribe is an exaggeration. It was a single shaman in the company of two younger Indians and a dog. Was hard to know the gender of the younger travelers at a distance and in the cover of understory as both sexes of local tribes wore their hair long and braided. The party was Algonquin, Paul told me, a band of Temiskaming displaced far from their ancestral lake.

"They thought of themselves as Anishinabeg, or 'true men.' Course, I didn't know that till later."

Algonquin translates to something like "at the place of spearing fish," which is appropriate as Paul was netting fish at an ice-cold stream when he noticed a set of unfamiliar eyes spying from a cover of oak and basswood.

He'd been observed for awhile. As did many tribes, the Algonquin revered the great spirit Manitou, that force of life or nature evinced in all created things, living or stone. Signs of the Manitou were everywhere; natives carried hairs of his moustache in totem, or a piece of birch bark carved intricately in the wake of some vision or dream. It was their reverence for

Gitche Manitou that gave these tribesmen reason to approach Paul and his mammoth bull.

"Though when I saw their bows and arrows, I was tempted to turn tail and run," Paul admitted.

Had Paul more experience he'd have known that the flints on those arrows were small and barbed for fish. He would have understood that the intricately woven containers slung on the warrior's shoulders were meant to secure the catch of the day, not scalps.

However, Paul had no such reassurance, so his caution was understandable.

These "Head of the Lake People" were, after all, among the Algonquins who at one time or another fought with both French troops and British, a weaving alliance of many bands reduced by pestilence and the Iroquois, and then by the encroachment of industry and logging. One of the younger men in black-dyed moccasins and buckskin trousers dropped his blanket to challenge Paul from across the water.

"Parlez vous Francáis?"

"... Oui," Paul answered with some reluctance. "Better with English, though."

For a moment it appeared as though that was the end of the conversation.

But then the shaman emerged to regard Paul frankly. The old man shuffling into the bright sun. Scratching his scrotum.

"You the trapper's son? The old man?"

"I am," Paul replied.

The elder muttered something to the young warrior at his shoulder who muttered something to the other warrior, and for a minute Paul wished he had his old man's rifle. The tallest of the young tribesmen took up the shaman's end of the colloquy.

"Grandfather says your animal has the Manitou in him."

"He's my ox. I'm not selling him."

The younger man translated and the old shaman spat.

"Only white man think he can buy the Great Spirit."

Paul tossed his net aside, and when he rose to his full height the Indians took a half-step backward.

"*Sacre blieu,* he is a giant!"

"I am sorry if I offended you," Paul called out, and then, grasping for some initiative. "May I share my catch? I have some bluegills, here. Pair of sunfish."

"We have not eaten," admitted one warrior.

"You bring the fire. I bring the food," Paul offered, and within an hour he and the Temiskaming were dining on blackberries and pan-fish.

Who'd guess that a chance encounter with displaced Algonquins would be the lens that brought Paul into the wider world? There were so many things he did not know, even near to hand. For instance, Paul had no idea how long it took to grow a tree. Fifty years? Sixty?

The old shaman shook his head.

"Tree in my village was there with my grandfather. And his before him. And him before his."

A tree could be centuries in the making, the medicine man told him; somehow Paul had not gleaned that knowledge from his logging experience. It had not occurred to the young logger that a felled tree might take centuries to replace.

"White man cut and cut," the shaman shook his head. "All the old men are gone. And their saplings, hah! No bigger than a woman's legs."

After the meal, Paul offered his net to the old man, but the shaman would not accept that gift without some sort of barter so he had one of the warriors give up a tobacco pouch in trade. It was a well-made pouch, fashioned of deerhide and finely beaded.

But there was one other piece of business left to discuss. A final exchange before the Algonquin parted company with Piotir's son.

"Do not castrate your ox," the shaman urged Paul in parting. "This winter will come and by next they will tell you he needs to lose his balls to be a working animal, but do not believe them. This animal has the Manitou strong. You take his balls; you take his spirit."

"Thank you, White Bear," Paul honored the old man's totem. "I will tell them Babe cannot be cut."

And he wasn't. His papa thought Paul was insane to suggest that a bull could be trained well enough to work the woods, but for the next two years Paul contracted himself out with Babe for small jobs along the lake and Babe the Blue Ox became known as one of the best-working animals in the north woods.

But only with Paul as teamster. It was three years after the

Babe was calved before Paul, now nearly twenty years old, returned to the Shallow Waters Camp following his enormous ox.

"I swear to God," Crosshaul confided to me later on. "If I hadn't seen Piotir at his side I wouldn't have recognized the son of a bitch."

By this time I'd quit my easy job at the Bronson Mill to sling ink and scale logs at the Shallow Waters Camp. We were well into the winter's season. I was shivering at my desk sorting time cards and schedules when all hell cut loose outside. I heard Crosshaul shout, "Oh my God!", and then Dutch Jake started cussing a storm, and I saw Red Murphy flash by faster than I'd ever seen that Irishman move. And then the dinner bell started clanging.

I hurried outside to see what was causing the commotion and at first nothing obvious presented. It's just Piotir bringing another team of oxen, I thought to myself. That's what it looked like.

Squinting my near-sighted eyes, I could make out our aging teamster and grinder half hidden behind a wide spread of horns, but even that impression was immediately confused as lumberjacks braving the cold in everything from trousers to longjohns descended en masse to greet the newly-arrived.

I thought to myself this old coot's getting a lot of attention.

Then I got closer and I saw that Poitir wasn't driving a team of oxen at all, nosirree. There was only a single animal harnessed to the Russian's sled, a bull ox, biggest bovine I'd ever seen, and off to one side stood this gorevan-haired fellah with a beard to his chest and tall as a damn tree. By this time every lumberjack in camp was carrying on like they were in the middle of a Methodist revival.

I saw Tom McCann practically run out of his homemade boots.

"The fuck is the ruckus?!" I yelled out.

"It's *Paul!*" Tom shouted.

"Paul—?"

I still didn't make the connection.

"*Come on, Johnny, it's the Kid. He's back!*"

And then I was yelling with everyone else.

"*He's back!!*"

Chapter Nine
Beaver Lake

Chance and perfidy combined to put me in the same crew with Paul Bunyan. The reason I was slinging ink and scaling tracts for the Shallow Waters Camp was that Swede Sturleson made sure I was fired from the Bronson Mill. "He's padding footage and getting kickbacks." The Swede went straight to the Old Man with that accusation. Of course, once a log is cut to dimension and sorted it's impossible to justify an initial estimate. It was pretty much my word against a timber baron's, and so I was not surprised one morning to find a bean counter waiting at my desk.

"Get your papers, Johnny. You're walking."

I had scaled for the Bronson Mill three years and was out on the street in three minutes. The lucky break was that Crosshaul needed a bookkeeper and was happy to have an inkslinger and a scaler for the price of one hire. I would remain in unbroken employment with Chris and his crew past the turn of the century, and shared camps with Paul off and on for another twenty years.

I'd been at the Shallow Waters Camp job maybe a month when Paul returned to the fold with his remarkable ox. Counting Babe, the camp had three yoke of oxen and four horses. Piotir was still double-dipping as the camp's teamster and grinder, but

Paul made clear he had not returned to be his daddy's gofer.

"If Papa needs help with Babe he'll let me know," Paul informed Crosshaul casually as he swung a broadaxe over his shoulder. "But I mean to work with the men."

Paul came at a good time and so did Babe. There was an enormous demand for timber and as I predicted the easy pickings along the Highland's rivers and tributaries were being rapidly depleted. By 1885 Canadian loggers along the Ottawa were having to go deeper and deeper into the forest for their deals, which put great strains on men and forest alike.

This was the period in which Paul came into his own as a logger and overall woodsman. There is a kind of hierarchy among lumberjacks. Fallers hold buckers at a slight remove. Buckers or sawyers hold themselves superior to bull punchers and snipers, and everyone holds himself superior to the boy greasing skids.

Paul was not like that. If the boss needed to swamp out brush for a skid row, Paul volunteered. While other fallers paused between trees to take a chew or grab a smoke, Paul bucked his own timber. If the snipers got behind he'd nose the logs, and nobody could take bark off a stick faster than Paul Bunyan.

He was a swamper, sawyer, teamster, and barker all rolled into one. Later on he'd become a high climber, gaining renown at the most dangerous job a lumberjack can do. And though Paul exhibited a low-key demeanor, his energy and initiative sometimes intimidated the older loggers. Brimstone Bill was a relatively new hire and after a day or two in the woods beside Paul that one-time preacher could be heard to complain that the boy was making him look slothful.

And then there was Babe. You hear all kinds of stories about Paul's ox. Most of them are downright silly. One tall tale, for instance, involves Babe and a tank wagon. Now, a tank wagon is just a wagon hauling water to ice a row of skids. The story goes that Babe pulled a tank so large that when it sprung a leak it flooded the Mississippi River.

There are any number of variations on this story: Babe pulling roads straight, Babe raising Lake Huron ten feet with a single piss. You get the idea. One story, almost lost, I think, has to do with a place called Beaver Lake. As were many frozen lakes, Beaver Lake was often used by loggers hauling sleds of logs to some landing or another. The story in brief goes that Babe pulled such heavy loads onto Beaver Lake that the ice broke, which was a real irritation, so Paul hitched up Babe to the beaver dam bounding the lake and in a single pull drained the whole damn thing to bedrock.

This is an exaggeration.

However, it is absolutely true that Beaver Lake, fifty acres of snow-fed water that for decades was home to beaver and trout and a meeting place for generations of Algonquin, was drained to rock in a matter of minutes. The carnage at Beaver Lake became embellished in shanty houses on howling winter nights all over the deep woods, but I was there to witness the real deal.

It was well into winter. Paul was twenty-two years old. He'd been back in the woods three or four seasons and was grown to his full height, which with boots was a smidge shy of seven feet. Babe had grown, too, an animal preternaturally large and strong and, in Paul's hands, as docile as a lapdog.

Babe was also extremely intelligent. Intelligence is not

something normally associated with oxen. In fact, you generally depend on an ox being dumb as six cans of paint. But any animal working logs has to be trained to a variety of commands in endlessly changing conditions, and it takes an animal with some smarts to master those skills.

Animals aren't born knowing how to accommodate sleds and yokes and swingletrees. They aren't born knowing to be aggressive on the uphill pull, but to hold back on the downhill slide. When Paul brought his uncastrated ox to camp there was real skepticism that he'd be of any use at all, but Babe fooled every one of us. That damn Babe was easier in the woods than most horses, and smarter.

On this particular morning Paul hitched his ox to a go-devil piled high with white pine to follow Piotir's sled down a narrow skid row to Beaver Lake. If you were a city dweller you'd say the day was cold as hell; for an axeman it wasn't too bad, probably twelve below, Celsius. Say ten degrees above, Farenheit.

Was hard to see the sky for the press of trees on all sides. A brilliant winter sun threw beams of illumination through the dense arbor in random javelins that sparkled on the crystals of an evening snow lodged in the boughs of spruce and white pine. The understory was as uncluttered as a Quaker meetinghouse. There was not a lot of wind.

I was tagging along behind the loaded sleds on a wagon filled with tools and provisions. My job that day was to survey the stumpage on the way to the lake, making an estimate of the feet to be culled and the cost involved. I guess it's pretty obvious that as loggers were forced to go deeper inland in their search for profitable tracts of timber, the expense incurred for every log brought to a mill went up. It took more men to swamp skidrows and build rollways. There were more landings to establish and many more to guard.

The miles got longer, Paul used to say, but the days didn't.

Anyway, Paul was right behind his *batya* when Piotir led his team of oxen out of the cover of the forest and onto the shoreline, some kid greasing the last skid poles along the way from a can of dogfish oil.

Now, Beaver Lake was located strategically between a pair of flanking bogs that were not only a bitch to get around, but dangerous. A man could be hip deep in quicksand before he knew he was in trouble, and even areas free of that hazard were too sammy to support the weight of a loaded sled. You could waste a lot of time detouring around those perilous swamps, or you could strike directly across the lake to the rollway on the far side.

It was the dead of winter, after all, and nothing is slicker than ice.

Of course, if it wasn't for the work of beavers, there'd be no lake at all. For eons, Beaver Lake wasn't much more than a healthy creek, a runoff for spring thaw, but over many decades beavers dammed that rill and in a few generations a couple of hundred yards of earthworks took shape that stopped the stream's flow like a tourniquet. Once that happened, the water backed up to fill the bowl upstream, and it wasn't long before instinct and Mother Nature engineered a large reservoir that in deep winter froze solid enough to support a team of oxen and a sled weighted with tens of thousands of pounds of logs.

In fairness I should mention that our push to Beaver Lake may have trespassed onto one of Swede Sturleson's tracts. We followed the runes as best we could, but it was not always clear where one section of timber ended and another began. We may have skirted The Swede's stumpage at some point, I still don't know.

I do know that days earlier Tom McCann warned Shot Gunderson that he'd seen some of The Swede's men on horseback near our landing on the far side of the lake.

"They been spyin' last couple of days," the Scotsman told Shot, who had retired his axe to become our bull of the woods.

We'd just chowed down and were back in the bunkhouse when Tom conveyed that information. Shot Gunderson was a good boss and cautious, but he couldn't very well stop work every time we got wind of Sturleson. Word passed around to keep a lookout for any sign of The Swede, and Gunderson suggested that Piotir might have his buffalo gun handy in case we needed to arbitrate some dispute.

We had spies of our own. Thanks to Paul, there were a few Indians in the area, mostly Ojibwe, who didn't mind getting salt pork and beans in return for keeping the camp informed of The Swede's whereabouts. But we had not seen a scout in days, and in any case by the time we reached Beaver Lake we had concerns unrelated to The Swede or his men.

Ice is never a sure thing. Anytime you're over ice with a sled full of logs, you're vulnerable. If the sticks roll, or if God forbid the ice breaks, you're in deep shit. The most common way to die was to get tangled up with the sled or animals. Dodge that bullet and you still had to get on top of the ice; ice can entomb a man as surely as timber.

But what if you went down in open water? This was cold

water, deathly cold, the kind of bath that snatches your breath from your lungs and numbs you to the bone, to the heart, even. If you've got a peavey and there's solid ice close enough, maybe you can get a bite and pull yourself free. Otherwise, the only way out is to be dragged out because you sure as hell aren't going to swim.

And of course once out of the water you could still die of exposure.

It was close to noon by the time we got our loaded sleds to the shore. We didn't see a soul besides ourselves along the way. I remember Paul scanning the far side of the lake, a pinch of snuff in his cheek.

"How's she look, Paul?" Gunderson asked.

"Nothin' moving. Red, you see anything?"

Those veteran loggers shook their heads. Then we spotted Dirty Dan waving his bowler hat from the distant shoreline and heard a muffled halooooo.

"There's Dan," Shot declared with relief. "Good. Coast is clear."

"Let's yard these logs, then," Piotir said, and with Dutch riding the runners the old teamster urged his team onto the ice.

Imagine a sheet of frozen water a hundred yards across. A brace of boulders along the strand was backed on three sides by sentinels of trees. And then on the downstream boundary the beaver dam rose up, an earthwork of mud and sticks holding back a wall of water. You could see Piotir's oxen pulling their enormous load almost effortlessly on a line parallel to that construction, the sled's iron runners biting into the lake's frozen track. Paul was about to put his sled on the ice when we heard the first explosion.

It's funny. You can bust dynamite a hundred times, but when you don't expect it, you're still not sure what you heard. It's like an earthquake; no matter how many quakes you've experienced it does not seem to register those first few moments why the pictures on the wall are swaying or why the silverware's dancing on the table.

But then a heartbeat after the first explosion came a second blast, and we saw mud and branch go straight up in the air.

"They busted the ice!!" the kid yelled and we saw Piotir scrambling to keep his team from stampeding.

"GET OFF!" Shot bellowed, and you could see Dutch and Piotir doing their best to oblige.

But then there came another sound, a slow, deep groan, and then a crack of black water thin as a hockey stick began to spider out from the point of the explosions.

A break in the ice getting wider.

"*Papa!*"

I saw Paul leap from his sled with a coil of wire rope.

"Shot, throw me a peavey."

Paul caught that tool and snatched a knife as long as my arm from his belt to cut Babe free of his sled.

"I need more rope, Johnny."

I was dragging a coil of rope from the dozen always stowed in the wagon. Shot barked an order to our greaser.

"Grab some line, kid!"

"Babe, back up. Back up, now," Paul commanded his ox, and I'll be damned if that animal did not back away from his sled like a collie.

"Haw, Babe."

Babe stopped his retreat and Paul threw a lasso over the ox's horns.

"*I NEED LINE, BOYS. FIFTY YARDS, AT LEAST.*"

"Jesus Christ!" our bull cursed as he scrambled to fetch more rope.

"All right, Johnny," Paul handed me a coiled line as calmly as though he was headed for a smoke. "I'm taking my end out to Papa. I'll need you and Shot to put together enough rope to reach. Make sure it's all tied off on Babe."

We had a line hitched to Babe, and Paul had a line for Piotir and Dutch, but we still had to rig a rope in between!

Fuck an A.

And who was going to handle Babe? Both our teamsters would be on the ice!

"Paul, what about Babe?!"

"He'll know what to do!" Paul yelled and without another word took off on a dead run across the shifting ice.

So there we were. Paul sprinting toward his papa and Dutch with a peavey in one hand and a coil of rope playing out from the other as Shot and I and a kid scared half to damn death scrambled to splice a connecting line.

Meantime Piotir and Dutch were in desperate straits.

"They cut the animals free!" Shot gasped, and you could hear the bellows of oxen pulled under the ice.

Piotir and Dutch were panicked, too. A man going into the water in winter was good for maybe five minutes. The stranded drivers had to stick with the sled; it was their only hope. They'd got free of the drowning oxen, that was crucial.

But they couldn't free the logs.

The sled alone might float, but not with a load of timber strapped on. That load could capsize at any moment, which meant that Piotir and Dutch were hanging onto a quarter of a million pounds of coffin.

Already we could see the sled listing over, more animals braying in terror as they disappeared beneath the ice.

And there was Paul jumping from shelf to floe like he was running logs. The ice *craaaacked* again, a terrible premonition. The sled tipped over and Piotir and Dutch disappeared beneath.

"*PAUL, IT'S TOO LATE!*" Gunderson yelled, but made not the slightest attempt to pursue the young man scrambling across the scattered floes.

"PAPA."

I saw a head pop above the water, and then another. Piotir and Dutch managed to climb the sled's runners back to the surface.

Thank Jesus.

But they were by no means out of trouble. By the time Paul reached the two men, they'd been in the water maybe twenty seconds. A minute more and they'd be too numb to grab the rope that Paul was desperately trying to throw over. Paul himself was in a different sort of mess, separated by a good twenty feet from Dutch and Piotir on a cake of ice heaving like suds in a tub.

"GRAB THE LINE."

Paul threw a loop of rope in a perfect lasso around his dad and hauled him over. Dutch came next. All three men were trapped on an uncertain island in the middle of rapidly breaking ice. I saw Paul slip a noose of rope under Piotir's arms, and then Dutch's. Then Paul grabbed a handful himself.

"BABE, GEE!"

Now remember Paul was a good fifty or sixty yards distant from his ox. There was ice busting and water churning and a dam tearing to pieces and above all that commotion, I am not shitting you, Babe heard Paul's command and without pause began backing up the skid row.

The line tied off on the horns snapped tight, and I saw Paul hanging onto Piotir by his coat collar as Babe the Blue Ox dragged all three men through shards of ice and freezing-cold water toward shore.

The boys were within a spit of safety and looked to be home free when the dam finally broke altogether. The whole mess gave way at once. The water under the ice burst through in a long roar and I thought for sure our boys were going to be swept downstream like chaff in an icy wind.

But the line held and so did Babe.

You could see Paul fighting the whole time to keep a hold

on his end of his frigid lifeline. One hand for the rope. The other to keep his father's head above water.

Beaver Lake disappeared, that much is true, acres of water crashing downstream in a wall of ice and mud that shook trees for half a mile. The logs followed, of course. Blind goddamned luck that the three men were not caught broadside by that crush of timber.

But they made it. Babe snaked Paul and Dutch and Piotir to shore like a snatch of sticks. Damn bull must've dragged 'em thirty yards up the row before we could get him stopped.

There wasn't a hell of a lot of time to celebrate. The loggers were out of the lake but by no means out of the woods. Here were three men soaked to the bone as the mercury hovered maybe ten degrees above zero.

"We need a fire!" Gunderson sang out, and the skid greaser jumped with me to soak a stack of kindling with dogfish oil.

I thought for a minute they'd all freeze to death, Piotir in particular. Here was a man over eighty years old chattering bad enough to shatter teeth and blue as a bird's egg.

We got a blaze going and fetched blankets from the wagon and did our best to dry the men off. Shot hitched Babe up to the wagon and took us all back to camp, the rescued teamster and the Dutchman huddled miserably beneath a pile of wool. We got back to camp and put the men in the cook house, Sourdough measuring out small cups of warm tea spiked with honey. Paul was doing all right, but Dutch and Piotir were in bad shape.

"Get me a couple pails of warm water," Sourdough told his bull cook and had the men stick their feet into those steaming buckets.

Finally Dutch quit shaking long enough to curse, and then Piotir settled down as well. But then the old Russian seemed to nod off, as though napping, and Shot jumped over.

"PIOTIR, CAN YOU HEAR ME?"

The old man smiled.

"I like to sleep."

"NO, PIOTIR!"

Shot slapped the old man across the face.

Paul didn't realize what was happening, but I did. The older veterans knew, too. They'd seen it before.

"Papa? *PAPA?*"

Hypothermia's very peaceful at the end, what I hear. Something like euphoria, even. We'd warmed him up, but the damage was done.

"Papa?!!"

Paul was by then shaking Piotir like a doormat.

"Let him be, now," Red Murphy admonished gently.

"Wake up! *PAPA—? PAPA?!!*"

The old Russian roused briefly. Looked up to find his foundling son.

"I am so proud to be your father," he said.

And then he died.

Chapter Ten
Pulling Up Stakes

I KNEW IT'D BE IMPOSSIBLE TO PROVE WHO PLANTED THE dynamite on the dam at Beaver Lake. Swede Sturleson denied any hand in the matter, which was to be expected, but it was hard to imagine who other than The Swede had motive to act with such purpose and malice. The loss of timber and animals was a huge blow to the Shallow Waters Camp but logs and animals can be replaced, given time and determination. Fathers cannot.

We had to go to Ottawa to find an Orthodox priest to sanctify Piotir's burial. Paul's father was interred in a pine coffin near his cabin not far from Source Lake. Elina stood by her foundling son during that graveside Mass, the mother if not the son embracing the holy mysteries of rebirth, renewal, and resurrection.

Paul was torn between a sense of responsibility for Elina and a deep despair over the loss of his father, those powerful emotions warring with a rage for revenge. Of all the people at camp in whom he might choose to confide, Paul risked me.

"I want to kill him, Johnny." Paul found me after the funeral. "I want to find Sturleson and rip his arms off."

"But you know you can't." I shook my head.

"Why?"

"The first reason, maybe the least important, is we can't prove The Swede's involved. He probably is, but you don't slaughter a man over probablies."

"That's one reason. What's another?"

"You're not Swede Sturleson," I tried to keep Paul's eyes in mine. "That man can bully or kill and sleep at night like nothing happened— he can. But you can't, Paul. And more important, you don't want to. You won't even shoot a deer, for God's sake, and that is a blessing too precious to lose. That is the way your papa wanted you to be and to remain.

"And what about Elina? Do you want your mother to see you become a man like Sturleson? I'm not saying you can't want revenge, Paul, or be mad as hell or sad or furious, but you do not want to lose your soul. Your mother would be crushed to see her fine young son piss away his gifts and talent over a son of a bitch as worthless and sorry as Swede Sturleson. And so would your father."

"I don't have a father," Paul replied bitterly, and as he left I realized there were at least two senses in which that was true.

The incident at Beaver Dam wreaked havoc on our camp, but Shallow Waters was not the only operation going bust. Between the near monopoly of Mr. Bronson's mill and the paucity of timber within reach of water, independent operators were going belly-up throughout the valley. And then, of course, Swede Sturleson's goons were everywhere. Jean Lafayette lost two rafts of logs when Sturleson's men released a sluice at the reservoir holding Jean's sticks. Jean tried to get credit from the mill to cover that loss for his next year's harvest, but was denied.

Speaking of credit, Crosshaul couldn't borrow money for a milkstool. His entire collateral consisted of six men, one ox and an anvil and when the boss convened his crew one supper to deliver that news, he was bluntly candid about his predicament.

"Boys, I don't have a pot to piss in, nor a window to throw it out of."

A glance around the cook house was enough to tell us that. The pine shelves were bare, sugar gone and coffee, too. We were saving tins of tea to sift three or four times, and we'd had nothing but wild game for meat in a week.

We couldn't meet our payroll, much less replace the equipment we'd lost at Beaver Lake or our livestock. Even if Chris could have borrowed the money, I wasn't sure there were tracts within two miles of the river worth harvesting. The Ottawa was about played out for small operators, but even the big boys would be looking for new stumpage by the turn of the century. We thought the supply of timber was endless. It wasn't.

"I talked with Jean Lafayette and some of the other independents," Crosshaul told his men, "and we all pretty much came to the same conclusion, which is, we either gotta fold or move."

By "move" our boss did not mean the usual seasonal dislocation. The only hope for operators like Crosshaul and Jean was to secure stumpage on U.S. soil. "There's still beau coup stands along the Fence River in Michigan," Crosshaul declared. "And the Pacific Northwest is openin' up markets for fir and spruce and redwood, too."

But for our first venture, Crosshaul was looking at tracts closer to hand.

"I figure our bet starting off is in Wisconsin," Crosshaul relayed that opinion. "Prob'ly along the Chippewa River is easiest. Fred Weyerhaeuser's done broke the mill owners' monopoly at Eau Claire and the Falls. They ain't no problem gettin' hung up at Beef Slough anymore, and there's no problem gettin' buyers neither. Way they got it worked out, the Mississippi River mills and the Chippewa River mills share the logs comin' down the Chippewa on a percent basis, an' they got more sawmills between 'em than Annie's got hoecakes."

Dutch Jake and Red spoke up to agree that it made sense to work along the Chippewa. The timber industry followed two basic transits—water and rail. Hardwoods like basswood and hemlock were prone to sink and so those logs were generally railed to the mills, but pine logs floated and the rivers and waterways in Wisconsin continued to be a sensible way to get timber and logs to buyers downstream.

The forests bounding the Chippewa Valley were rich in white pine and the Chippewa River fed directly into the Mississippi. In addition, major operators were laying down narrow-gauge tracks deep into the woodlands. You could find railheads blooming like wildflowers, so whether you followed steel or stream you were in pretty good shape.

Not a man on our crew kidded himself it'd be an easy trek. We'd have to find our own agents and our own stumpage. And this was a dislocation involving technology as well as geography. Loggers in the States had become much more productive in the years after their Civil War. It wasn't that they worked harder or drank less that gave the Yanks their edge.

It was their love for machines.

Mechanized cranes and loaders made sawmills models of efficiency everywhere, but the Yanks pioneered a new breed of locomotives that brought those contraptions deep into the forest. The Shay was an early example, a steam engine that pulled steam-driven loaders on narrow-gauge rails to logs felled miles and miles inland. However, even that matrimony of steam and steel did not revolutionize the lumberjack's life nor end the age of horses and oxen so surely as a primitive wood-fired winch called a donkey engine.

A model of simplicity, the early donkeys used a one-cylinder steam engine linked through a rudimentary clutch and transmission to a capstan wound with steel cable. Donkey engines come in about the same variety as cats, but all donkeys have these things in common:

They are easy to operate.

They are unbelievably durable.

You could manage a donkey engine with three men and a boy. A punch operated and maintained the engine itself. A setter received the donkey's cable and mated it with a choke chain snugged around the butt of whatever log was waiting to be snaked in. You needed a horse and rider to pull the donkey's steel cable out to the setter. And then you needed a whistle punk.

A whistle punk enabled cutting crews to communicate with the punch managing the donkey. Logs could be felled a hundred yards or half a mile from the donkey, way too far for shouted instruction. A light pull line solved that problem, a simple cord that ran from a steam-vented whistle at the donkey engine to crews down the line.

With various combinations of short and long whistles, you could signal snags or breaks in the line, or emergencies. You could let the punch know when to take up slack on the line, or when to back off. Was typically a boy who was responsible for relaying these signals, and every time the whistle punk jerked his cord he risked killing somebody.

It's not hard to see why. A logging cable is a ten-thousand pound bullwhip, a lash of steel that can take out trees or men for fifty yards on either side of its pull. If a whistle punk signals too soon, a choke-setter loses a hand. Whistle too late and a logger half a mile away gets cut in two.

Most operations required more than a single donkey engine. Depending on the terrain and the size of the tract, you might have half a dozen donkeys working at intervals, one crew passing logs along to the next donkey up the line until you finally reached a railhead or river.

This was the age of machines, for sure. Babe the Blue Ox was already an anachronism. But machines cost money. So do men and cook houses and bunks and the rest, and Paul's camp was broke.

"Wisconsin's waitin', boys, but we can't move without a stake." Crosshaul settled his doughboy frame against the cookhouse table to deliver that verdict. "I know we got the heart and the guts for the job, but unless one of you meadowlarks has got hisself a gold mine, I don't know how we can finance a logging camp anyplace."

That provoked some back and forth. Sourdough declared he could always find work. He'd just take his bindle-stiff south and "hire out as a gyppo." Red Murphy hated that prospect.

"Work a day here, a day there, camp to camp? That's no life." Red turned to Crosshaul. "But you're sayin' it's either that or no work at all?"

"About the size of it."

That's when Paul surprised us all.

"Maybe we can work for each other."

"The fuck?" Dirty Dan spit into a bean can. "The fuck does that mean?"

"I don't have a gold mine," Paul said. "But Papa did leave me something. I talked with Mama. She agrees we should use it for the camp.

"But not for any one boss. If we go south, we go together. We take our wages after profits, and we don't make a dime till every bean is counted and paid for. Johnny can help us with that."

"I can't buy beans without cash or credit, Paul," I replied. "I'm an inkslinger, not a magician."

"Nor a bank robber, I reckon," Shot growled, and everybody kind of laughed.

Paul just smiled.

"But what in hell could Piotir have give you that can help?" Crosshaul asked Paul. "'Cause I can tell you for sure, we're gonna need more than a damn buffalo gun."

"More than a buffalo, for that matter," Dutch punned but this time nobody laughed.

Paul waited for us to settle.

"How much money do you think we need, Crosshaul?" he asked.

"Well, lessee. Assumin' we can scavenge every blanket and peavey we got here, and assumin' every man brings his own equipment, I could prob'ly get by with a thousand, maybe fifteen hundred dollars Canadian. I'd have to borrow against 'bout half of that, of course. Call 'er an even two thousand. Why? You got two thousand dollars, Paul?"

The loggers roared laughter with that. Two thousand dollars! Might as well ask the kid if he had diamonds up his ass!

"I have what Papa left me," Paul said and bent down to pull a gunnysack from beneath our cook house table.

It was just a water-stained sack of burlap, but when he hefted it, you could tell there was something substantial inside, something of bulk.

Paul set the bag on his knee and reached inside and then he pulled it out so we all could see—

A Bible. But this was an old book of Scripture, you could tell that at a glance. It was more than a foot thick, and the cover looked like it was as much wood as leather. There were fantastic illustrations scrolled all up along the spine, gargoyles and demons mixed in with the Virgin and Her Son.

"The fuck, Paul? You want us to pray for a stake?"

"No, no." Paul smiled affably. "Though I don't guess that would hurt. No, what I mean to do with Papa's Bible… is sell it."

Then he opened the tome, and we all 'bout dropped off our logs or stools or slop buckets or whatever it was we were sitting on, because when Paul parted the covers, we saw that each page was completely framed inside a slender boundary of vivid art. The margins of every page were filled with scenes from Genesis to Revelation, delicate wreaths of symbol and picture bringing to life parables and personalities from man's fall to his redemption, the sins of man captured with startling candor along with the Stations of the Cross.

The wisdom preserved on the Bible's hand-lettered pages was largely lost on the Shallow Waters Camp. But there was another value everyone could see, the most vulgar of virtues, perhaps, and also the most obvious. Everyone in the cook house recognized that Paul's Bible was illustrated in filigrees of solid gold.

Chapter Eleven
On, Wisconsin!

It took a couple of weeks to sell Paul's rare book of Scripture. Big Ole just could not understand why I contacted an appraiser in Alberta to help find a buyer. "I can haf her melt in an hour," Big Ole groused. "You can have yer gold before chow."

The book was worth a lot more than its gold leafs, as it turned out. A curator from McGill University bought it from my Alberta connection for a little over three thousand dollars Canadian, which meant that, even taking out the middleman's commission, Papa's Bible gave his son an inheritance of more than two and a half thousand dollars.

Paul turned that money over to Crosshaul, and as word spread, other independents contemplating an exodous to the States made bids to join our operation. We must've talked to a half dozen camps, but in the end Jean Lafayette offered a thousand dollars plus equipment to merge with the Shallow Waters crew and Crosshaul accepted that offer with Paul's blessing.

By late August we'd consolidated our camps, packed our gear, and caught a barge across Lake Michigan to the Wisconsin shore. Jean Lafayette brought along two wagons to match our single cart, along with additional tools, lines, and naval stores.

He also brought along another eight or ten lumberjacks. "Be much more better to have twenty men than ten," he told Crosshaul.

Everyone knew that Piotir's gift to his son had given us all a second chance. Some of the boys even said we should make Paul a bull of bulls, since it was his money financing our newly expanded crew of loggers, but the kid would not entertain that idea.

"Jean will be our camp bull. Crosshaul's bull of the woods. Johnny's got the books and payroll."

"What about you, Paul?" Jean inquired.

"I got an axe and an ox to handle, which is more than enough work for me."

We reached the Wisconsin shore and with Babe the Blue Ox pulling our three loaded wagons headed south in a column for the Chippewa River.

We had what we needed to build a logging camp, everything from Ole's anvil to Sourdough's skillet, but none of that matters if you don't have trees. I'd already telegraphed ahead to have a timber cruiser meet us at Jim Falls. Larki Jay rendezvoused with us about the middle of the week. He was a Finn, turned out, a short, dark fella with a seaman's cap and leather trousers who took me and Paul and Jean Lafayette by horseback to a tract of white pine located between the Falls and Eagleton.

It was a paradise of white pine that'd never been touched, trees straight as masts without disease visible from horizon to horizon. I also spotted at least half a dozen other evergreen species that improved the landscape with leaves and bark of delightful variety. I saw balsam fir between the pines, that bark smooth and gray. Jack pine was common near lakes and sloughs in that forest, and red pine was prevalent in stands scattered throughout. I also saw white and black spruce, red cedar in great numbers, and hemlock.

We were at around a thousand feet of elevation with manageable grades on all sides and there were uncountable numbers of streams and tributaries all about. But we were miles from the Chippewa and deep in the woods, far from any railhead, which meant that the cost of getting our harvest to market would be higher than our operation in Canada. I asked the timber agent how much it'd cost me to lease a tract close to a railhead.

"Enough to buy a Shay, grade a line, and put down tracks," the Finn replied. "The timber barons here are in bed with the railroad barons. They don't like small operators."

"That's all right," Paul dismissed that jibe. "We'll make do. Now Mr. Jay, what are you gonna want for this stumpage?"

There are two basic ways to acquire a given tract of timber. You can pay for the whole kit and caboodle up front if you're Diamond Jim Brady, or you can defer payment based on delivery of logs at a negotiated price per unit. I was given a power of attorney to negotiate on behalf of our camp, but we were short on green, which the agent had to know when he first laid eyes on our ragtag caravan. That meant I'd be haggling over a price linked to some unit of production.

I might open with a bid for, say, a nickel for every thousand board feet received at the mill. I've seen contracts based on cords of wood or even by the ton, but generally price is based on every thousand feet delivered to the mill.

Larki proposed a variation on these themes.

"I want a thousand American dollars up front," Larki declared. "Plus ten cents per thousand."

"Mr. Jay, I am astonished."

"Why's that?"

"Because apparently you can get blood from a turnip."

"Suit yerself." The agent shrugged.

"Tell you what." I cleaned my glasses on my sleeve. "Why don't you strike up a camp with Paul here and let me scale this timber?"

I took my pencil and some paper and rode the woods for the rest of that day. I was back by nightfall. Paul had caught some fish and was listening to the Finn going on about his parents in the old country, herding reindeer and such.

"My mother is a Finn," Paul remarked.

"Where is she?"

"Ottawa now. I found her a place."

"Must cost a pretty penny."

Paul smiled. "We had a Bible."

I draped the reins of my horse over a laurel bush and proceeded to take off the saddle.

Larki glanced over. "Well, what about it, scaler? What do you think she's worth?"

"A nickel per thousand is all right," I replied. "But if you think I'm payin' more than a couple of hundred up front, you're mistaken."

The three of us sat down over a mess of rainbow trout and a pot of coffee and pretty soon acquired our first stumpage in the States at six cents per thousand feet and a three-hundred-dollar bribe. I signed the contracts by campfire and paid the agent his front money out of my saddlebag. The only thing left to do then was to get hold of some donkey engines and a punch to run them.

Thank God for the railroad. We moderns in 1920 take steam engines and other conveniences for granted. You want a piece of equipment from Portland or Sacramento, you can telegraph to a dispatch or put in a paper order, and within a week you've got your snatch block or clevis pin or writing desk or whatever you need. And we have banks to forward credit and cover checks and purchase orders, not to mention cash transactions.

Nothing was that celeritous in 1888. I first telegraphed a supplier in Oregon, who replied two days after my inquiry that I could expect delivery in four to six weeks. But then reading an Eau Claire newspaper, I saw that an operator had three used donkey engines for sale. It took four or five days, but we got the donkeys delivered at a railhead near the falls. The problem then was to get the machines transported to our newly got tract west of the Chippewa.

Fortunately, the boys at the depot were Johnny-on-the-spot. "Tell you what," the dispatch told me. "We've got loaders here can put those donkeys on one of our flatbeds. There's a spur leaves here that connects with a railhead serving a narrow gauge out to the Steuben Camp. I can call Mr. Steuben and ask him about taking on your donkeys at the spur. They got a Shay can bring your engines to within a couple of miles of your tract. Can you get 'em in from there?"

I thought about Babe the Blue Ox.

"I can," I said.

"Good." We shook hands. "That'll be another twenty dollars for me. And maybe another Jackson to sweeten the deal for your neighbor."

This was how business worked in those days, and in that respect, come to think of it, things haven't really changed.

By early September Jean Lafayette's men were working alongside the Shallow Waters boys to build a bunkhouse, cookshanty and barn. Before the first snow we'd swamped out skid rows and landings and roughed-out or repaired at least half a dozen sluices at reservoirs on tributaries feeding the Chippewa River. Paul teamed up with Jean and two of his men to build the rollways that come spring would release our sticks for the drive downstream.

Our camp was located near a tributary the boys dubbed Round River. Folks hearing Paul's name mentioned with Round River nowadays are likely to be reminded of a yarn that's grown over the years. Story in brief is that Paul and his men were driving logs for days and days on the Round until somebody finally noticed they kept coming back to the same place they'd started from. Takes Paul a while in this telling to comprehend the river is circular.

A figure of brawn rather than breme.

I can report with confidence that Round River is not round, just as Whistle River does not whistle, though Onion River as you might surmise, was named for a particular weed redolent in the vicinity. In each case loggers coined a name or appellation, usually based on some local characteristic. Round River, for instance, is notorious for its convoluted twists and turns and could just as easily have been designated the Blacksnake River or the Tornado.

And lumberjacks nickname people as often as places. In fact, a logger is more likely to be known by a sobriquet than by his Christian name. Shot Gunderson never revealed his given name to me, not even for the payroll. Neither would Jean Lafayette, though Jean did admit he adopted his nom de guerre after some trouble in Chicago. Something about a warrant for assault inspired that revision.

Jean brought ten loggers and a donkey punch to Wisconsin and not one of 'em went by the name his mother gave him. Curly Charlie was the cherub-faced newcomer hired to operate our donkey engines. Curly got his moniker, as you might expect, from an untamable mop of hair that he stuffed under a derby hat, but we also called him Fat Angel or sometimes Short Hand, which was mean-spirited as Curly had actually lost a hand years earlier when his shirtsleeve snagged a cable on a donkey's spool.

Loggers love to make light of any misery, especially someone else's. Crosshaul declared at the cook house, and in Curly's presence, that he had doubts about hiring a man who could only handle his tool with one hand. Dutch Jake expressed sympathy with that assessment, adding that with Curly on the job they'd always be shorthanded. Curly told them both how the horse ate the cabbage, and there was a good laugh all around.

In the end, Crosshaul hired Curly, and I tell you what, that was one of the best calls he ever made because Curly Charlie was a damn genius when it came to anything mechanical, a regular grease monkey.

"He kin take a donkey apart and put it back together with one hand tied behind his back," Jean assured us.

"And which hand would that be?" Crosshaul inquired drolly, but hired the man anyway.

We picked up our steam-powered winches at the railhead, delivered as promised. Curly was there to make sure we weren't sold a bill of goods. Once our punch was satisfied the donkeys were in fair condition, we had to offload the contraptions from the flatbed to our own wagons. Lucky for us, there were a couple of loggers waiting to catch a ride back to the Steuben Camp. As Crosshaul said, and once again in Curly's presence—"We need all the hands we can get."

It's not an easy job dragging cast-iron engines off a flatbed, with the concomitant attachment of boilers and winches and five hundred yards of steel cable, when you don't have steam-powered cranes or loaders. However, with a couple of blocks and tackle and some ingenuity we managed.

Course we couldn't have done it without Babe. Was ironic that we were now depending on an ox to offload our donkey and tow it back to camp, but mating Babe to the simple physics of pulleys made the job almost easy.

Three days later we were felling trees. Paul got up with the other men around four thirty in the morning for breakfast in the cook house. The bell would clang for breakfast and then once again around five, which sent the boys out to the woods.

We had three engines and three crews pretty much set up as usual but Paul would not have any youngster at whistle punk so Shot took that responsibility for one engine, and Jean Lafayette pulled one of Sourdough's bull cooks along with an injured man to punk the other two donkeys.

I wondered those first few weeks how the Shallow Waters men would get along with Jean's newcomers. Jean's men, after all, had got a paycheck for their winter's work, whereas the Shallow Waters crew had lost an entire season's earnings at Beaver Lake. That kind of disparity can create problems in any camp, beyond the usual frictions bound to crop up in such intimate circumstances. It helped that we had a fantastic cook.

I am talking about Sourdough Sam, of course. That irascible genius of wilderness cusine. You hear about a woman getting to a man's heart through his stomach? That adage, with very little modification, goes in spades for a logging camp. It's especially difficult to get good grub in winter camps. Not like you're going to have fresh tomatoes or rhubarb pie in February. Some camps virtually lived on beans and salt pork; try that diet for two months straight and you're guaranteed constipation and revolt.

When asked why his own crew was so tractable, Paul pointed to his taciturn cook and said—"Ask Sourdough. Nobody pans a cake like Sam, and he can make a caribou taste like stockyard steak."

That praise granted, a camp feeds on leadership as much as johnnycakes and wild game, and in that respect I was not sure that Jean and Crosshaul would make good partners. These were men who were very proud, who'd never failed at anything, and yet The Swede had beaten them both. They also were not owners anymore; they were partners with Paul in a tricky arrangement that held no guarantee for success. But within a few days it became apparent that Crosshaul and Jean held each other in genuine respect. It's not that they never disagreed, but they never squabbled in front of the crew and they never showed rancor at the cook house. Loggers notice that sort of thing.

A good camp sets standards, whether at the teapot or at the cross-saw. Jean was our lean and compact camp boss, and Crosshaul was our well-fed bull of the woods. These were both good men, but there was no doubt in anyone's mind that Paul set the example for the fallers and buckers and punchers. He was a force of nature, and when you woke up at four thirty and it was black dark outside and colder than a witch's tit in a brass bra, Paul was already leaving the barn, the breath from his lungs frosting on that fiery beard as Babe the Blue Ox trailed behind as obediently as a collie.

Paul set the example in the forest. He was our bull of bulls.

Of course, it took Paul, Crosshaul, and Jean all together to manage the score of men at Round River, and each man contributed in different ways. For example, a good boss needs an excellent and ever-varying fluency with profanity. A good boss also can't be afraid to use his fists, and he has to know when to use them. In this respect, Chris Crosshaul might be underestimated, a soft-framed, moderate kind of fellah. Not even prone to raise his voice. But I remember one time at supper, Smiley Andersen, who never smiled, started a rukus at the table. Something about taking another man's seat. Crosshaul strolled over and knocked Smiley flat on his ass.

"Nobody owns a seat," Crosshaul growled.

A boss also has to keep an eye out, or a nose, for liquor. There is always alcohol in a logging camp. Half the time if the cook house runs short on sugar, it's because somebody's got a still. A bad boss will bust the hooch; a worse boss lets the men stay drunk; a good boss strikes a balance. Jean actually encouraged beer at supper, but would not tolerate a snoot on the job.

It should go without saying that when you're supervising lumberjacks, you're dealing with big people possessed of even larger personalities and that's where an intimate understanding of your crew pays dividends. Crosshaul knew that Dirty Dan had a trigger temper, for example, so for the first few weeks he paired Dan off with Tom McCann, the camp cobbler known among other things for his bright-blue ascots and even keel.

Even with those sanguine indicators I was worried. Winters test any crew, and the wood gods, as everyone knows, are capricious. At first, my worries seemed unjustified. The Round River crew did not squabble amongst themselves. They did not spend the nights in their cups. They did not quit or flag. Jean Lafayette said he'd never seen men work so hard, and Crosshaul agreed. That crew of men felled more timber in a single day than they ever managed at their Canadian camps. The boys yarded more logs in a week than they ever had, and all without a single paycheck.

It would be tempting to give Paul credit for spurring that kind of effort, and in fact the cutting crew did just that. The stories of Paul Bunyan and his ox that circulate today are proof of his popularity at Round River. And there is no question that Paul's example, not to mention his skill, strength, and endurance, made men work harder and longer than they otherwise would. That is true. But it is also true that the main thing improving the pace of work in Wisconsin and later on in Michigan was not a man at all. It was a damn machine.

The donkey engine made normal men supermen. A donkey can winch five times the load an animal can pull, but more importantly a donkey also snakes logs to the landing a hell of a lot faster than any team of animals, which meant the boys with saws and axes had to bust their butts just to keep a single donkey busy.

Paul challenged the machine by challenging himself and his men to compete. The kid would place bets against his own day's quota, or he'd match his day's fell against two or even three men at a time, dropping trees sunup till supper. Other days he'd take the two-man saw, picking loggers at random to partner.

Have you ever actually seen a tree fall in the forest? If you were swinging an axe or pulling a saw, would you know when your tall pine or spruce or fir was about to crash to the forest's floor? Loggers do not have prepared runways to avoid renegade trees. The ground all around is mined with branches and tools and other entanglements, and so you have to give yourself time to escape. A split second's hesitation is the difference between a calm retreat and death.

In the early years, a logger's work was confined to the winter season, and so very often the first thing to alert those fellas that a fall was imminent was snow. Whether you're using an axe or cross-saw the tree will shift when it's close to breaking, and when it does flakes of snow dislodge from the branches above, a gentle drift of icing.

Just a few flakes at first. But then the topmost branches begin to sway back and forth, back and forth, as if caught in the caprice of wind, and that oscillation becomes more violent second by second until the craaaack of release as some spruce or pine crashes to the forest floor.

The tree falls and with that impact snow bursts like shrapnel to pepper the lumberjacks, crystals of frozen water hanging in a cloud that may persist for minutes at a time. In that span of moments and in treacherous footing, a bucker de-branches the tree and cuts it into manageable lengths, a choker snugs a chain around the butt and secures the cable, the punk whistles down the line, and as the log snakes toward the landing the fallers already have their cleats and spring boards into the next tree destined for human construction.

"Fucking near killed me, he did," Red Murphy declared after a day chasing the donkey with Paul. "Best day I ever had in me life."

We had loggers competing every way you can imagine, man against man, team against team, Monday's cut over Wednesday's—it just got infectious. The camp kept up the pace through October and November and things looked almost too good to be true. Christmas came and went without a major accident or setback, and by spring we had sticks stacked behind rollways up and down that twisting river, just waiting for the spring thaw and a head of water for a drive to the Chippewa and the mills beyond.

We called ourselves The Round River Boys, and the camp enjoyed the best morale I've ever seen. Work was hard, but so was play. I'd drop by the bunkhouse after a day's tally and find Jean Lafayette with a fiddle and home brew as Red Murphy donned a kerchief and dress to sashay with Curly.

Or maybe it was the other way around, I forget.

And the boys loved their ditties. You don't need a fiddle to sing, and lumberjacks have a set of lungs, don't they? I can remember approaching the bunkhouse leaning into a blizzard, yet even in that howling wind I could hear the roughneck choir inside. I'd guess half the songs were about some girl or another.

"Peggy Gordon" was an old standard and "Barbara Allen". One of Sourdough's crumbs, oldest man in the camp, actually, would sing "Annie Laurie" like an altar boy and then reminisce about his time in the Crimean War, singing to Annie in the trenches at Sevastopol. Those nights were lively.

Other nights the shanty would be quiet as cribbage. You'd go in and there'd be a pot of tea on the woodstove or sometimes coffee. Some logger'd be down to his skivvies darning socks or Tom'd be filing the spikes on somebody's boots while somebody else was writing a letter or dictating to somebody who could write. Those were the evenings you could get yourself a game of checkers or cards, though the rule in the woods was you never on any account played for money. Matchsticks, but not money.

The men worked six days straight from dark to dark in a constant bid to beat the previous week's cut. Every man was looking forward to a good paycheck come spring, and the only omen I could see threatening to darken that bright horizon—

Was Paul Bunyan.

Small things got my attention. Take the horseplay in the bunkhouse, for example. Now, granted, I don't bunk with the boys and I don't see 'em every night, so it took me a while to realize that everybody took his turn at the buck dance, or singalong or fiddle—except Paul.

Loggers don't trust a man who's stand-offish. Paul wasn't superior at all, in that sense, but he wasn't social either. Sometimes when the boys were cutting up, I'd see the kid slip on his boots and buckskins and slip outside, out in the wind and cold.

"The accident changed him" is how the old-timers explained the behavior to the new men on our crew. "He was just a kid and it was malicious an' it nearly killed him. And then The Swede took his papa."

As Doc Murphy warned it wasn't just a matter of healing bone and sinew. With Piotir's murder, Paul seemed to lose interest in anything not directly related to trees and axes. In fact, it seemed that he lived for nothing but work.

It was hard to say whether his bunkmates noticed Paul's reticence. Paul remained as polite and hardworking as when he was a kid at his father's side. He never complained, and he listened to every man's counsel with an open mind. But every now and then you'd catch Paul leaning on his axe or against the bole of a tree, his face empty of any expression.

Of course, those moments of reflection or retreat or whatever they were did not come often. Most times, Paul affected a bemused countenance that stayed the same whether the subject at hand was a cup of coffee or a snake bite. It took me a while to realize that the giant in our midst hid behind a mask most of the time, and in moments where the bunkhouse was rowdiest, Paul was most opaque.

The boys would be fiddling and singing and without preamble or excuse Paul'd leave their company. Now and then I'd grab my pipe like I was going for a smoke and trail Paul outside. He never went far, just down the skid row to the tree line was about it. He'd drag over a pole to sit or sometimes find a stump. If the weather was clear he'd spend half an hour just looking up into the sky. Other nights, he'd pull out his jackknife to whittle some little thing or another.

I must have tracked him out three or four times when, without raising his eyes from his carving he challenged me.

"Somethin' I can do you for, Johnny?"

I felt ridiculous. Like a kid caught robbing candy.

"I just was worried is all," I replied lamely, and he smiled.

"You don't need to worry, Johnny. Not about me anyways."

"Well," I tried not to sound defensive as I paced over, "it's just I notice that when the fellas are having a good time you generally look for a way out."

"It's no trouble," he replied deadpan. "We got a door."

"That's not what I meant."

He regarded me for a moment.

"Know what you need, Johnny?"

"What's that?"

"Place for your pipes."

"My pipes?"

"Red's got a rack for his'n. You need one, too."

"I don't have anything like Red's inventory."

"Still," he folded his knife. "I bet I could make somethin'."

It wasn't long afterward that I came back from the cook house to find on my desk a pipe rack hand carved from the heart of a red cedar. Paul took a whole tree just to make a holder for my nascent collection. An entire tree felled for a trifle the kid could have whipped together from kindling. I accepted the rack that Paul made for me, and I've used it ever since, though not always to stash pipes. But I remember thinking at the time that a gesture so unexpected and extravagant was an unsettling omen.

Chapter Twelve
The Round River Drive

GENERALLY SPEAKING, A LOGGER CAN EXPECT AN INTERLUDE of a month or so between the business of cutting trees and the drive to the mill. By the first of May we'd felled most everything worth having, and had piled or boomed a small fortune of white pine behind rollways and dams built to catch the spring flood that would push our logs from Round River to the Chippewa.

The dams were spaced like landings on a stairway to catch the coming headwater. Once gorged, Paul and his crew would open the dam gates in sequence and sluice the logs into the driving water. It wouldn't be long before the river overflowed.

Would the booms break?

Would the dikes hold?

I brought the boys some coffee sometime before midnight.

"Much obliged." Paul finished his in a gulp.

It was a beautiful evening, but still chilly, cakes of ice floating amidst the silver logs like lilies in a pond. There was frost on the ground, too. I remember the sound the boys' spikes made as they trudged along the dam's periphery, like a crunch of crepe paper. But that was about the only sound coming from the Round River crew. There was no horseplay. No small talk.

We'd already seen signs of the coming torrent, brush, mud and debris ripped loose by the headwaters raging upstream now surging past with floes of shattered ice. It was close. You could feel it. You could smell it. Every man on the dam was itching to bust the gates.

To ride the raging river.

"Take your time, *mon ami*," Jean Lafayette cautioned, and Paul lifted his chin to acknowledge.

Both men knew from experience that logs released too soon from their spill would outrun the river's flow and jam downstream. Paul would need to release some pressure off the dam before cutting our sticks free. He cocked an ear upstream.

"Won't be long."

The headwaters hit around one that morning, raising a foam like some gargantuan head of beer. The ground trembled with the river's rout. And the roar! You'd have thought we were perched beside a cataract! Paul's crew held the logs just shy of the dam's spillway as he opened the gate, and a wall of water burst out like a ten-cunted cow pissing on a flat rock. An hour or so later, Paul finally turned to Jean Lafayette.

"I believe she's ready."

"Run 'em."

Paul picked up his pike pole and nodded to a man we'd got from Jean's Canadian crew.

"All right, Nasty, it's you and me."

Nasty Staponski was actually "Nasti" Staponski, a fun-loving Pole in his thirties who did not in any way share Dirty Dan's aversion to tub baths or soap. Nasty left a slaughterhouse in New York while still in his teens to find more congenial work in Canada, and by the time he joined Jean Lafayette's camp was already a seasoned hand.

Staponski loved being a river pig. Once selected, he stagged his overalls with a bowie knife, bragging how he'd best any driver in white water. This was no idle boast. Nasty had sluiced logs for many years. He was as steady on floating timber as a dancer on a stage. But anyone who's tried to direct logs through the gates of a fast-spilling dam knows that it only takes one shift of current, one missed step, to screw the pooch.

Nasty had his pike pole in hand and was working only yards from Paul. The conditions were good; there was hardly a breath of wind and the moon though high was full. The logs drifted placidly in our dammed-up pond, their boles pale as the humps of whales. Nasty had already herded a dozen sticks through the gates when Paul sent him another.

"Comin' yer way."

Jean's man backtracked on his own log to intercept a thirty-footer headed for the spill and when he shifted his footing, just a simple shift of weight, the stick he was riding rolled out from under him.

I never will forget the look on his face—more surprise than fear, really. As though he were merely startled.

"Shit, Ma!"

And then he went under.

"NASTY?"

Paul bellowed.

"NASTY!!"

The logs closed over the Polack's head as surely as the lid of any coffin. Nasty went under, and the last thing I saw was his face, a startled lily in an ice-cold pond.

The body would not be found for days and by that time the men who knew Nasty Staponski, those who had felled with him or sawed with him, or cut cards with him, were well distracted downstream. There would be no memorial for the Nasti, no day of mourning or grief, though now and again the boys would debate whether it was better to be crushed by logs or to drown.

Folks hearing these things are sometimes unsettled to see how little time lumberjacks take to pay respects to their fallen mates. How callous, people say. How cruel. But what are you supposed to do when a man dies and the gates open and the logs are moving? What are you supposed to do when a man goes down in the same moment that ten, twenty, or a hundred thousand sticks jam at a bend or waterfall?

The river won't wait. The logs won't wait. Scant moments after Staponski lost his footing, Tom McCann joined Paul to launch stick after stick through the gates and down a sluiceway white with foam.

"HERE WE GO, BOYS!"

Imagine the boom of a cannon in a cave; that is the sound logs make when they pile *en masse* onto a spring-whipped river, and once the sticks hit you are moving on instinct, a cowboy caught in a never-ending stampede. You cannot pause. You cannot reflect. You are a splinter riding a storm.

A man could cry his heart out in that tumult and never be

heard.

There would be time later on to remember. Paul and the other drivers would recall Nasty during some respite for food or sleep as they waited beside a dam for the headwater to build. They'd take tins of tomatoes from their nosebags and with a cup of hot tea tell stories as loggers are apt to do.

But I suspect if you were present at a hundred campfires and heard tales recalled of a hundred lumberjacks killed in the forest or on the drive, you'd soon realize that the yarns bantered over those disparate soirees sounded pretty much the same.

"He was one crazy fucker." Red Murphy remarked over a pipe, as Dan broke out a fiddle and Tom McCann mended yet another pair of boots.

The boys would smoke a pipe or hoist a jar of home brew to that crazy Polack. They might even indulge in some lugubrious ballad or another. But then it was back on the river to a carpet of seething timber, and in a week or a hundred miles Nasty Staponski was truly gone forever.

We made the Chippewa without losing another man and over the following weeks Paul and the other drivers never set foot off the raft that was their floating bunkhouse. I followed the crew's progress from ashore with Chris and Jean, restocking provisions for the boys as needed. It was smooth sailing all the way to payday, except for one lightning storm that threw a bolt straight through the raft's galley. Sourdough said he'd never seen bacon so crisp.

We had a buyer waiting at the largest booming works in the United States. Beef Slough ran for at least fifteen miles, a calm of water located just north of Alma along the eastern bank of the Mississippi River and stretching northeast along the southern bank of the Chippewa. Mill owners along the Chippewa used to war with owners along the Mississippi over the rights to logs coming from upstream. That squabble was settled with a compromise that let sawmillers purchase a pre-set percentage of timber routed to Beef Slough.

An enormous boom swung out into the river like a gate to divert our raft and countless others off the Chippewa and into an eddy of protected water. Beef Slough was around fifteen miles long, I reckon, every mile of it lined with gaps and pens constructed to receive millions of feet of floating timber. I was on the fins of the river-boom admiring the sweep of river and commerce when the Round River pigs brought our raft off the Chippewa.

"HULLO, FELLAS!"

I met up with Crosshaul and followed our raft to its assigned pen. It took hundreds and hundreds of men to manage the gaps and pens and booms at The Slough, with scores more employed to strap and bind the purchased logs into brails for transport down the Mississippi. I'd never seen so many human beings working in one place, but even in that swarm Paul stood out. The tenders working the log-pens were used to seeing haggard and exhausted lumberjacks at the end of a long drive, but a tired giant was new to everyone's experience.

"Good to see you, boys," Crosshaul greeted his crew as they stepped off the raft, making sure to shake each rough hand. "You look like shit."

"Look better with some green in me pocket," Red spoke up, and Chris told him we'd be meeting our money man later in the day.

"Meantime, why don't you go on over to the Union Hall in Alma?" Crosshaul suggested. "The other boys're there already. I'll catch up with you when things are settled here."

Jean Lafayette was waiting at the ferry for our bone-tired drivers. Paul stayed behind with Crosshaul and me to make sure our logs were properly scaled and also, of course, to receive payment for product duly delivered.

"Be damned if I don't believe that's our man."

I turned to see two men strolling toward us through the pens. The gentleman wore a four-in-hand tie with wool slacks and a suit-coat; I could see a scaling stick stuffed into the satchel hanging heavily in his hand. The other fellow was stepping lightly, a short, dark-skinned ringer in frayed trousers and a sailor's hat.

"Mr. Inkslinger?" the gentleman called out.

"Yes, sir."

"Bob Rutledge here. From the Clinton mill."

I expected to meet the buyer's representative, but I sure as hell didn't figure on seeing Larki Jay. But there he was, squinting at our pen of logs below the narrow brim of that cocked hat.

"You checking up on us, Mr. Jay?" I jibed.

"I had my doubts," our timber agent replied, "but that's not why I'm here. I was just a couple of pens down to sign off on a delivery when some tender started goin' on about a redhead eight feet tall with shoulders wide as a moose-rack. Well, hell, they ain't but one of those around, and I figured wherever the kid was, you couldn't be far behind."

"I suppose you'd like to get paid."

"That'd be splendiferous."

"Let's get these logs scaled then, shall we, Mr. Rutledge? And we can all leave happy."

When the bark sheet was tallied to satisfaction, Mr. Rutledge walked Crosshaul to the office and made payment in cash for a little over seven hundred thousand board feet of white pine. Even with the pay due our loggers, and fees paid to the boom operator and timber agent, there'd be money left over. In fact, the camp made enough profit on that drive to pay Paul back every dime of his investment, had he let us.

But Paul didn't want to do that.

"Just put her in the kitty," he said when Chris rejoined us at the pen. "There'll be more where that came from."

Larki Jay on the other hand was happy to collect his fee from Crosshaul's moneybag, promising as he left that he'd have virgin tracts for us in the coming year.

"You boys are making a name for yerself," Larki declared, and I'm not sure that without that prompt I'd have noticed that Paul was drawing fresh attention. You'd see a head turn or hear some guarded comment. Finally one of the tenders edged over, an older man who came just about even with Paul's belly.

"'Scuse me," he said. "Don't mean to interrupt yer business."

"No, sir," Paul replied. "Not at all."

"It's just, we ain't seen anyone your size before. 'Cept maybe in a circus or a freak show, and them boys wear boots."

"Well, truth to tell, I'm wearin' boots myself." Paul smiled, and the old man laughed like it was the funniest thing he'd ever heard.

"What's yer handle, young fella?"

"Paul will do."

"Well, I tell you what, Mr. Paul, the ladies in Alma have got themselves somethin' comin'."

"I hope so," Paul came back and you could see tenders and boomers chuckling all around.

It embarrassed him some, I could tell.

"Think I could use a pipe."

Paul opened his bindle and pulled out a corncob smoker along with a pouch intricately beaded with shells and stones, and immediately a gap-tender nearby stopped in his tracks.

He was an Indian. You couldn't mistake those highcheeks and burnished skin. He was soaking wet from the tip of his raven ponytail to the soles of his well-spiked boots and shaking like he'd seen a ghost.

I first thought, Well, it's just another yokel never been around your average Samson.

But it wasn't Paul that caught the native's attention. It was the tobacco pouch.

"Want a smoke?" He extended the pouch and the Indian shook his head.

"Been working the Slough long?" Paul asked.

"Long enough."

Paul dipped his pipe into the pouch as the Indian shivered in the breeze.

He seemed to be debating some course of action.

"What is it?" Paul prompted.

"Your pouch. Is it Ojibwe?"

"Yep. Traded a fish-net for it. Why?"

The Indian worried his pony-tail a moment before replying with another question.

"You ever seen a blue-hided bull?"

Where the hell did that come from? I looked at Crosshaul. He looked at me. Paul did not seem the least perturbed.

"I own a bull-ox some call blue," Paul tamped his bowl casually, and in that instant the native's face went pale as a Presbyterian.

"I got to work," the tender blurted, and before any of us could reply he leapt from the pen to land like a sparrow on the logs rolling below.

"The hell was he about?" Crosshaul asked as we all leaned over the rail, but the Indian was nowhere in sight.

Chapter Thirteen
Dream Weaver

It wasn't long after Paul spooked the Indian that we boarded the ferry with our bag of earnings to join the remainder of our crew in Alma. In a short while we were on the Mississippi where brails of timber crowded alongside scores of vessels engaged in all manner of commerce. Following the wake of a tugboat dubbed the *Percy Swain,* Paul and I counted a dozen barges not related to the timber industry, huge floaters and hoppers hauling everything from quarried rock to bundles of willows. We spotted three quarter boats and two building boats as well, these last no doubt headed for some dam work on the Big River.

But Paul was most taken with vessels not related to industry.

"Over there," he pointed and I saw a paddock of floating homes moored along shorelines. These were paddle drivers, for the most part, double-decked palaces riding the gentle wake of passing traffic. We saw a woman in a long, linen dress leaning out a window of her waterborne home to tend a flowerbox rioting in marigolds and daisies, brilliant spots of domestic ease.

Paul shook his head. "Now I seen everything."

We found the shore and hailed a carriage. Alma was a town nothing like Ottawa, a modest center of businesses and commerce strung below a bluff above the Mississippi. You could probably walk the whole burg in twenty minutes. Driving up Church Street you got a feel for what life looked like away from the riverfront.

Church Street took us through a community about as different from a logging camp as could be imagined. The ruts we followed ran between tall rows of maple and birch that shaded hardened sidewalks on either side. Framed houses and bungalows looked out to kids running on new spring grass, mothers at the stoop with neighbors or engaged in distaff labor.

"It's so quiet." Paul shook his head.

Everything was clean and permanent. We saw a horse pulling an enormous barrel of water on an iron-wheeled wagon.

"What's he do?" Paul asked our driver.

"Waters the street," the man answered with the knowing arrogance of an urban dweller.

"To keep the dust down," I amplified.

Paul smiled. "Reckon we could get 'im to douche our bunkhouse?"

"Couldn't hurt." Crosshaul chuckled and our driver sniffed.

He'd obviously seen his share of lumberjacks or smelled them.

"Take us down to the Union Hall," I directed our driver, and within minutes we'd left the somnolent streets on the outskirts of town for the bustle of commerce.

The hall was located near the Alma mill, that concern a confusion of wood and iron located toward the end of a muddy street that was thick with telegraph lines and two-storey buildings of varied construction. Within a year the mill would burn to the ground and take most of the adjacent businesses with it, but on the day of our visit the street was noisy with millworkers, tradesmen and lawyers dodging horse shit and horse-drawn wagons in constant perambulation.

We'd barely quit our buggy and paid our driver when I heard somebody ask if that was the kid in the Wild West Show? I tried to imagine Paul standing next to Annie Oakley, the axeman and the sharpshooter side-by-side like a barrel beside a bonnet.

The Union Hall was an aging brick and mortar building with iron grates bolted over the windows. You breached heavy oak doors to enter a hallway graced with a linotype of Eugene Debs and a poster for suffragettes, exactly the sort of announcements you'd expect to find in a nest of wobblies.

I peeled off a couple of bills for the toady out front and followed Crosshaul and Paul up a well-worn stairway. We entered a room with long lead-paned windows looking out to the carryings-on below, the mix of bustles, bowlers and brogans.

You could see everything from rags to riches on that muddy boulevard, but the only pockets our boys cared about were their own. Everybody from crumb boss to cook was eager to see his take for the season, and I have to tell you it felt good to come back from Beef Slough with cash in the bag.

"Goddamn," Red Murphy swore. "Been so long since I had a dollar in my hand, I forgot what it feels like."

Of course, it was a safe bet that with Red's habits he wouldn't be feeling it much longer. Loggers have a reputation for boom and bust, don't they? But I have to tell you, most of the crew that time around were smart enough not to take the whole kit and caboodle at once. They'd be raising hell that night and were smart enough, most of them, to know that if they left a loaf with me and got rolled later on in some whorehouse at least they wouldn't be broke.

There wasn't a lot of smalltalk at that payday. I checked the time on my log, gave every man his earnings and he was out the door. Slam, bam, thank you, ma'am. Didn't even change their shirts, most of 'em. Finally the only folks left were the bosses, Paul, and me. And Sourdough Sam. Our cook was not inclined to follow Red's antics or Dutch's.

"First season and we made a profit," Crosshaul declared grandly.

"Yes, we did," Jean agreed. "And in good shape, too."

"Except for Nasty," Paul chided.

"Kut haf been vorse," Sourdough came to Jean's defense and Paul smiled.

"Well, gentlemen," I spoke up to change the subject. "Are we drinking? Out to a show? Do they have shows in Alma? Or what about a hot meal?"

"Why not do it all?" Jean replied and at that moment I thought we'd got home free.

There was no show in Alma that would interest lumberjacks. For that sort of thing you'd go to Eau Claire. This was a town where everybody rubbed shoulders, which was fine by me. I didn't want the boys getting into too much trouble.

Jean took us to a hotel off the water that offered catfish and crawdads along with beer and beef and mashed potatoes. We found our rooms and bathed or at least sponged off and changed shirts and underthings, and then convened downstairs to just about eat the place out.

That was a pleasant span of moments, a long table pulled up next to windows looking over the river. We four had a couple of nice ladies and an older matron in aprons and high collars serving the table. Was incredible to get food that did not come from a tin or a sack. Even Sourdough offered his compliments.

"Dees ees velly gut."

Smells are erotic and there was an ambrosia of sensuality at the table that could not be avoided. Imagine the smells of beer and butter and home-made bread. The perfume of lilac water and clean clothing. This was a hotel about as chaste as a boarding school, but no man could ignore the promise of starched muslin or the swell of a breast as the girls leaned over to put down platters of biscuits and pitchers of stout.

One of our servers, the youngest, could not take her eyes off Paul, and who could blame her? Even sitting, he was taller than she was.

She kept finding excuses to attend him.

"More butter, sir? Or bread?"

"Mary," the matron warned.

"It's all right," Paul came to the child's defense instantly, instinctively. "I'm gettin' used to it."

There were at least eight or ten tables as well fixed as our own, with teams of locals and lumberjacks filing in and out. Jean Lafayette was offering cigars toward the end of the meal and I was about to settle up with our hostess when I saw Paul freeze at the end of the table.

I turned around to see what'd got his craw, and there was the Indian. The gap tender we'd crossed at Beef Slough.

Paul pushed away from the table.

"Paul—" I tried to stop him, but he just shook his head.

I didn't know what to expect. The Injun could've had a knife or pistol. I half suspected he was crazy, and I was pretty damn sure he hadn't got to our hotel by accident.

The fuck did he want with Paul?

About that time, Paul leaned over to the serving girl.

"Mary, is it?"

"Yes, sir."

Paul directed her attention to the redskin.

"Have that man over."

"But, Mister, we don't serve Indians."

"You don't have to serve us. Just find a table. Here."

The kid slipped her a dollar.

"The hell is goin' on over there?" Chris Crosshaul chortled. "Paul got 'im some jelly roll?"

"Somebody he met at the slough is all," I replied with a confidence I did not feel.

"Should one of us be handy?"

"I'll go." I made that decision and pushed away from the table. "You boys enjoy your cigars."

Paul was out of the dining room by then, but by following

Mary's return, I was able to backtrack him to a table that was actually outside, on a verandah facing the alley. He'd taken a barrel to sit across a cutting table from the native.

"Paul—?"

"It's all right." Paul seemed to be saying this for the Indian's benefit more than for mine.

"What's he want?" I asked tersely.

"My tobacco pouch, at the moment." Paul nodded and I saw the Indian tamping tobacco from Paul's pouch into a pipe that looked to be carved from hickory.

"*Merci.*" The tender handed the pouch back to Paul who filled his own corncob pipe.

"Join us if you like, Johnny."

"Don't mind if I do."

I produced a briar added to my rack in a trade with Red Murphy and presently you could add a tincture of tobacco to the other bouquets competing for attention.

"Say your name is Whitefeather?" Paul leaned back on the wall with that question.

"Frank Whitefeather," the Indian nodded.

"You Algonquin, Frank?"

"Ojibwe."

"We ever met before?"

Whitefeather took a long, slow draw to consider that question.

"Never met, no," he said finally. "Not before Beef Slough."

"How'd you know about Paul's ox?" I broke in.

"All the tribes know," he shrugged, and then ignored me entirely as he returned to Paul.

"He is your totem," Whitefeather declared.

"Babe?"

"The bull ox, yes. Your gift from Gitchi Manitou. You did not take his balls, then?"

"No, I followed a shaman's advice in that regard."

An enormous wave of relief seemed to pass over the slightly built messenger.

"You all right, Frank?" Paul inquired patiently.

"Yes, yes," the Indian replied. "But my grandfather had a dream. You should hear it."

Paul assented with a nod.

"Grandfather said that in the dream there is a dam of beavers on a lake…"

The hell? I felt a crawl over my skin. Paul seemed unruffled.

"It is winter. The lake is frozen. An old man follows a sled piled with logs and a pair of oxen onto the ice. It is not far to cross. Maybe two long throws of a stone.

"But in the dream there is a man with a bearskin coat and silver dollars on his hat, and he stands over the dam and breaks it with his boot. The old man and the sled, they fall into the black water, and that is where the dream ends."

I did not move a muscle. I was afraid to twitch. Paul remained quiet a long moment. Then he took a pull from his pipe. When he exhaled, the smoke caught a breeze and vanished in tendrils on the wind.

"I respect the Manitou, Mr. Whitefeather. And I appreciate the power of dreams. No doubt your shaman is a powerful seer. But this was not his dream."

The Indian averted Paul's steady gaze.

"I don't know what you mean."

"I mean that this is your vision. You were at Beaver Lake. You saw my papa on the ice, with the logs. You heard the dynamite."

Whitefeather shook his head.

"No. It is worse than that."

"Worse!" I exclaimed. "What could be worse than that?"

"I did not just see the dynamite and hear it," the Indian replied. "I set it."

"Mary and Joseph!" I gasped and resisted the impulse to get between Paul and his papa's killer.

Paul, however, seemed completely composed, if grave.

"Did The Swede tell you to do it? Swede Sturleson?"

"He had me set the sticks and cap. He told me it was to drain the lake. I did not know he meant to take your logs until the fuse was lit."

"You're claiming Sturleson fired the fuse then?"

"He ordered it," Whitefeather replied. "He was watching

from the trees when the old man came with one other. The fuse was laid inside the dam. You could not see it.

"But it was another white man put the match. A tall white man with a scar on his scalp and a ponytail like mine put the match from the tree line."

"Hel Helson," I grated and Paul nodded.

"Should have killed that son of a bitch when I had the chance."

"You don't want to be an outlaw," I objected, but Paul seemed oblivious to that caution. He leaned forward on the barrel. You could hear the staves creak with his weight.

"And what do you want from me, Frank?"

Whitefeather spread his hands on the well-knicked table.

"The dream. My dream. It will not go away."

"You needed a job, didn't you? The boss gives you a task. You do it. You couldn't of known it would kill my papa."

"But it did kill him!"

Whitefeather ground the water from his eyes.

"That's when I saw the blue bull. When he pulled you out with the old man and that other."

The Indian put down his pipe and sighed.

"I am in your debt," he sighed heavily. "How must I pay?"

Paul glanced over to me, but I had no idea what to suggest. This was brand-new territory to me. Paul then took his pipe from his mouth and tapped out the bowl on the heel of his boots.

"Tell me where Sturleson's been. Tell me where I can find Helson."

"Paul, do you think that's a good idea?" I clamored.

"Tell me."

Whitefeather raised his eyes to meet Paul's.

"The Swede was here three days ago, at Beef Slough." Whitefeather squirmed in his seat.

"He's logging down here?"

"Not yet." Whitefeather shook his head. "But he's planning."

"How do you know?" Paul asked.

"Because I heard him talkin' to that timber agent, the Finn. The Swede says the Ottawa Valley is played out. Cut to matchsticks, he said, and then he asked Larki Jay what the prospects were in the States, and Larki told 'im there's good stumpage in Michigan."

"Why should we trust you?" I asked pointedly. "How do we know you're not here to finger Paul? Is that it? Sturleson's paid you once. Why wouldn't he pay you again?"

"He's not here for money, Johnny."

Paul pocketed his pipe as he shoved up off the barrel.

"Where're you going, Paul?" I asked. "What'll you do?"

"I got dreams of my own," he replied.

Paul left Frank Whitefeather with me on the porch, and I knew then that dark days were coming.

Chapter Fourteen
Dark Dreams

The summer is a season of indolence for loggers. A time to get fat and lazy. A time for summer girls and summer dreams. The Round River boys would not gather again until the fall. I held over at Alma, taking a room on Church Street, and lost track of Paul altogether, and his ox. Big Ole paid me a visit around the Fourth of July and said he thought "the kid" (as Paul would always be known to that cadre) was back in Ottawa to take care of his mama. Gretta Hertz found Elina a house for widows, a nursing home we'd call it nowadays.

I just hoped Elina was the only person Paul planned to take care of. If I fretted about The Swede's intentions in the United States, I was petrified about Paul's under any flag. The nameless anxiety I'd endured the previous year, the sense that things were too good to last, crystallized with Frank Whitefeather's revelation. It was one thing for Paul to suspect that Swede Sturleson was responsible for his father's murder, but another thing altogether to have eyewitness proof.

What would Paul do? How would he react? I had no idea what to expect, but with the change of seasons, I found out. By summer's end, I'd negotiated another contract for stumpage on Round River. Larki Jay was happy to seal the deal for a section scaled at somewhere between twelve and fifteen million board feet of white pine.

"You can get rich on this one, Johnny," Larki told me.

"Heard there's lots of folks acquiring stumpage."

"Shaping up to be a good year," the agent agreed.

"Heard we had some Canadians looking. Fellah Sturleson was down here. You know The Swede?"

Larki folded his copy of the contract into his jacket.

"I never talk about another man's business, Johnny."

I didn't press. I had worries apart from Swede Sturleson. First thing we had to do was greatly expand the size of our camp. As the leaves turned glorious in their autumn plumage, we built three new camps along Round River. Jean brought down two more gangs of men for a total of fifty-three lumberjacks, and I had Curly Charlie purchase four new donkey engines for what we all expected would be a rip-roaring season.

Autumn turned to winter and Paul showed up late, which did not endear him to either the veterans or our new hires. Red and Dutch and Dan were bulling gangs of their own, busting their tails dark to dark by the time Paul walked into camp. The rookies had been swinging and sawing right alongside the seasoned jacks for two weeks, and you could see sparks off Big Ole's hammer from dawn till dusk. Every man looked to be pulling his weight—except Paul Bunyan.

Even after he got to camp, Paul never fit in. I'd see him pass by and it was like watching a wraith, a shadow. He almost never had a word of greeting to offer, never anything like conversation. Just that sad, absent smile.

He moved out of the bunkhouse. The excuse was that he was just too damn tall to fit in a muzzleloader, but nobody believed that nonsense. The barn became Paul's personal crib, and Babe was his only valued companion. I walked a mule back to the barn after supper one evening and there he was, stretched out in a stall next to his bull-ox.

"Johnny," he offered laconically.

"Paul," I replied, and nodded to the mule.

"He'll want some water."

But Paul seemed indifferent to that need so I managed the task myself.

The veterans were willing to cut Paul some slack, but the newcomers saw his eccentricities as indulgences and were constantly chafed that Paul was favored in work assignments or other accommodations. Jean and Crosshaul spent more time than they wanted to cajoling the new hires to accept Paul's solitary contribution.

"He still does the work of three men," Jean pointed out.

But Paul decided what work that would be, and he almost never helped anyone else. We'd have five donkeys and five crews yarding logs while Paul'd be off with Babe dragging in a solitary stick.

He was no longer a bull of bulls. In fact, he didn't bull anything. He didn't encourage other men. He didn't take part in the friendly competition to increase the day's cut or yard. He even took meals on his own, brooding over stew and beans in the barn or else out in the tree line.

The whole tenor of the camp changed that second season. You didn't hear the fiddle or the slap of checkers on a homemade board. We had accidents. Dutch Jake put a peavey through his foot. Some Canuck lost his fingers to a blasting cap. And the old Brit who survived Crimea got tagged by a rattlesnake and died. A snake bite? In October?

Slights that should have blown over festered into full-blown feuds. Curly said the next man gave him shit about his missing member would be sucking one closer to his crotch. Red Murphy and some punk working the donkey were about ready to duel over a hand of cards. By Thanksgiving, Jean and Crosshaul agreed it was the worst gang of men they'd ever been around. They also agreed with me that Paul was a big part of the problem.

"What do you think we should do?" I asked Jean and Chris one night in my one-room inkslinger shack.

Jean exchanged a glance with Crosshaul.

"Well, I hate to say it, but… I think we should let him go."

It might seem foolish to fire the best lumberjack in North America, but we didn't need a prima donna in the woods or even a superman. We needed a logger who could bring the best out of other men. That was what made Paul really special; that was what got the tall tales started. It was the love of woods and woodsmen that made Paul larger than life, not his boot size or his ox.

And now that was gone.

He was terse. He was surly. He worked when he wanted to work and quit when he wanted to quit. I was there one afternoon when a cable got snagged and sheared off the donkey's drum, leaving logs scattered over a quarter of a mile. Red and Dutch and the new boys were scrambling to make repairs as Paul plodded by with Babe.

"Say, Paul, a hand here?" Red called out beneath the load of three tons of cable.

Paul kept going as though he hadn't heard a word. And maybe he didn't. Maybe Paul didn't hear or see anything that winter that wasn't right in front of his face. I guess nowadays you'd say he was depressed or had a breakdown or maybe he was shell-shocked. That's what he acted like. Like a doughboy just out of the trenches.

"He's not helping us and he's not helping himself," Crosshaul worried. "And it all started with that damn redskin."

"That's not entirely true," I qualified. Paul's demons predated his conversation with Frank Whitefeather. As Paul admitted, he had dreams of his own.

Thanksgiving came and went, and by December we'd lost four more men. They weren't killed or injured. They just walked in, told me to make out their papers, and left. The bull cook stuck his head in right after.

"Jean wants you at the smithy."

I hurried over to the blacksmith's shanty and found Jean and Crosshaul waiting.

"We've got to do something," Jean declared without preamble.

We were behind in our cut and with the worst of winter ahead everyone knew what had to be done. Everyone could see the elephant in the room. Jean Lafayette was about to announce his decision when a shadow filled the door. We looked up from the glowing kiln and there was Paul.

"You don't need to do anything."

He scuffled his boots along the dirt floor.

"Make her out. I'm quittin'."

It was Christmas Eve, 1889. Paul was twenty-three years old when he left Round River with his bindle, buffalo gun, and blue-skinned ox. He didn't say where he was going or what he planned to do. Over the next few years we'd hear stories, fantastic accounts of a red-haired Goliath at logging camps in Minnesota and Michigan or sometimes the Northwest. Tall tales they've come to be called. But I would not see Paul again for more than a decade, and until I took his testament in 1920 I did not know how he faced his demons or conquered them.

I did not know the darkness of his dreams.

Chapter Fifteen
Tall Tales and Tiwanah

Laboring in my cramped quarters to recreate the arc of Paul's life, I realized how little I knew of his exile in North America's forests, so what you get here comes from rumor as well as memory. Be warned that when it comes to Paul Bunyan, rumor can be more accurate. It's not that Paul would lie to me; it's just that memory is pliable, especially under stress or challenge, and Paul was not exactly introspective in those years or systematic in the record of his activities.

He sure as hell didn't keep a diary.

But piecing together what Paul told me decades after the fact, and mating that information with what I've heard over many years from other loggers, I am confident that the broad outlines of his Michigan odyssey are accurate. For example, I know there was a logging camp at Farrell Dam on Pine River that was bossed out of Menominee, Michigan, and I'd heard the story about the barn, the burning barn.

Certainly it's true that the season after he left Round River, Paul gypped out as a teamster for Jimmy Knox, who was the camp bull at Camp Two on the Pine River. Jimmy was a camp bull by the time he was twenty, a little bantam rooster of a fella, but he was excellent with maps and transits and generally regarded as a fair boss. Mr. Knox actually needed a faller more than a teamster, but Paul wouldn't let anybody handle Babe but himself, so Jimmy let him team Babe and a stable of probably twenty horses. Well, one day while Paul was out yarding logs, Larki Jay paid Jimmy a visit. Seemed the Finn had a buyer with ready cash willing to take over Jimmy's tract.

"Not interested," Jimmy declined. "There's good timber here, and I aim to harvest it."

"You might want to consider the man's offer," the sailor-capped agent persisted.

"You haven't even told me the man's name."

"Been asked to keep that confidential, Jimmy. Kind of under the table like."

"A man wants to stay under the table don't sound like a man I'd wanna sit with."

"It's Swede Sturleson."

"Ah. Thought that sumbitch was up Ottawa way."

"He has been, but you know them Canadians. They're all comin' down."

"All the big shots, you mean."

"They pay good money, Jimmy."

"Not to me they ain't. Tell The Swede we ain't no competition. Let it go at that."

Larki left, and Jimmy didn't pass along the day's conversation to anyone, including Paul, and why would he? Paul was not a principal at Pine River; in fact, he was only about two rungs up from a crumb bull. He was a day hire, a gyp. It was his job to take care of the livestock and the barn in which he slept. Jimmy didn't know anything about Paul's history with Sturleson, and even if he had I doubt it'd have occurred to him to confide Larki Jay's veiled warning.

Was probably a week after the Pine River boss rebuffed Larki Jay that the camp's barn became a pyre. Paul was taking Babe back to camp when he saw the smoke. Here's Paul's recollection.

"I roped Babe off and ran the rest of the way into camp. The barn was wrapped in fire. Rolling in it. There was men runnin' in with buckets of water, but it was like pissin' on Hell.

"I couldn't get within ten feet of the barn door it was that hot, and even that close you couldn't see a thing for the smoke. Couldn't see my hand in front of my face, it was that black. But you could hear the fire. And you could hear the livestock, too.

"That was pitiful. Horses screaming, kicking the paddocks. One or two busted out, but most of the stock was burnt with the barn and that stench hung in the air all winter."

Fourteen horses were immolated. Two mules made it out but were so badly burned they had to be put down. Paul used his papa's rifle to end that agony.

No one at first, not even Paul, connected the fire to Swede Sturleson. Jimmy Knox wrote it off as a terrible accident, most likely the fault of some half-hooched Indian. In those days there were always a few stragglers from local tribes mingling at camp with tinkers or panhandlers out of work. You went missing an axe, or a pot, or a pair of socks, Indians were the easiest to scapegoat, and Jimmy was inclined to hold "the natives" responsible for any such aggravation.

There still remained scattered remnants of the Ottawa, Potawatomi, and Chippewa tribes who frequented the camp where Paul was employed. These natives came ostensibly to trade for chewing tobacco or potware or occasionally a rifle. That sort of barter petered out quickly, and yet the Indians returned. Finally, it became apparent that these visitors were not nearly as interested in trade as they were in Paul's blue-hued ox.

"I don't know what kind of medicine the Injuns saw in that damn bull," Jimmy cussed, "but Babe was for damn sure what kept 'em comin'. They'd drift into camp around sundown just to see Paul walk that ox in. Wouldn't be long 'fore you'd see a jug passed around."

And since Indians and whiskey don't mix a lot better than loggers and whiskey, Jimmy felt justified to blame redskins and alcohol for his loss of barn and livestock.

"Was prob'ly one of them Injuns did it," Jimmy grated. "They come under a pretense of tradin' pots and skittles, and next thing you know they're drunk as hell and making whoopee with that fucking ox. Their totem, they call him. I should never've let Paul bring that animal to camp."

Jimmy notified his superintendent of his suspicions, and a couple of government agents rode out to speak with the local tribesmen, but nothing much came of that. Meantime, the camp needed new draught animals. Jimmy forked over good money to replace his stock, and Paul was sent to make sure they were delivered safely.

"Jimmy gave me a purchase order for fifteen horses and a mule," Paul told me in one of our late-night conversations. "I picked up the animals at Pembine Junction and shipped 'em over the Soo Line to North Crandon. I paid the freight charges out of cash Jimmy gave me, but I had to build a stock chute to get the animals off the car. The depot at North Crandon didn't have a ramp for offloading livestock.

"Anyway I got the horses down and corralled off so I could pick up the supplies Jimmy wanted, and after that I got my team for the drive back to camp. It was February, colder than a well digger's ass and I'm about a mile from camp when I see an Indian with a squaw and little ones sittin' on pine needles in the lee of some overhang or another, nothing but a blanket and a papoose between 'em, frying a scrap of rabbit or some such over an open fire.

"They were in bad shape, you could tell that. The squaw kept coughin' into her blanket. I stopped long enough to leave off some beans and salt pork out of the stores I'd picked up and the old man asked me if I worked at the Farrell Damn camp and I told him I did, and he asked if I'd seen the blue ox there, and I told him I owned the ox called Babe, which information seemed to brighten his lights.

"As I left, though, I warned the old brave that Jimmy Knox didn't want natives at camp anymore and explained about the barn. The old warrior just shook his head. 'Was not my people,' he told me. 'It would offend our spirit to harm a living thing in that place. The camp is sacred ground on account of the ox. A gift of Gitchi Manitou. He lives in our dreams.'"

Paul left the elder and his family, promising to return with provisions. He teamed Jimmy's newly acquired animals back to the Farrell Dam Camp but for the next few days was too busy raising a barn to worry about a squat of Indians.

"We didn't see any Injuns at camp after the barn burned down," Paul insisted to me. "And we didn't see 'em nearly as often in the woods as we used to. But they were there. I'd leave a croker sack of victuals or panware by the skid row and next morning it'd be gone. And every now and then I'd be setting a choke on some log, and I was sure somebody was watching. You could just feel it. Of course, I know now it was Tiwanah's people."

Tiwanah's people were Potawatomi, a tribe that along with the Ojibwe and Chippewa were descended from even more ancient forebears, but that shared heritage did not insulate her band or others from fierce competition. The Menominee, for instance, had taken sturgeon along the river named after their tribe for generations until Chippewa downstream thwarted the sturgeon's migration upstream with a series of basket dams.

The son of a chieftain related matrilineally to a woman in Tiwanah's band traveled south to negotiate a compromise with the Chippewa and was roasted alive for his trouble. The Menominee went on the warpath in the wake of that incident and Tiwanah's tribe was dispossessed of their own hunting grounds in the carnage that followed.

"It was about a month after the barn burned that I saw her," Paul recalled. "It was winter still, and I'd busted some ice on a stream feeding the Pine so's Babe could get some water. I remember my hands being raw in the wind, and I'd lost my hat and all I was thinkin' about was getting back to the barn for a smoke.

"But Babe needed waterin', and just about the time I got him situated I noticed a kind of fog twining up through the boughs of a basswood on the far side of the crick. Looked like a mist curling up, and then I realized there wasn't no snow hanging to the branches, nor ice neither.

"Then I caught a smell of sulphur an' I knew then it weren't no fog rising; it was steam drove up from a hot spring set on the creek. Just a small rock bowl bubblin' alongside that frozen run, right across from where Babe was drinkin' his fill.

"I couldn't remember the last time I'd had me a hot scrubdown and was contemplatin' a detour for that purpose when I saw Tiwanah get up from her bath.

"Her head came up first, sneaking up from the water like a cormorant, that hair dark as soot. I couldn't help watchin'. She splashed some water on her face and then stepped up out of the pool, and I saw a mane of hair black as crows' wings and falling past her butt.

"She stood there in that warming mist without a shell's worth of shame, and I was 'bout thunderstruck. I'd never seen a woman stand naked like that, not even in a whorehouse. She was tall. Tall as most men. Breasts small, like pears. A flat belly and wide hips. I bet you could leave a spoon on her hips, and it wouldn't fall off. And her skin was perfect as a fawn's, smooth and rich. Like fresh cream in a cup of coffee.

"She spotted me pretty quick, but it didn't seem to spook her none. She looked me right in the eye across that frozen stretch and by God I knew I had to find a way over. I told Babe to back on out—"

But in the span of seconds it took the ox to lift his head, Tiwanah was gone.

Vanished in a fog of fiery vapor.

Chapter Sixteen
The Company Cooler

Paul worked Mr. Knox's camp on the Pine for another two years before moving to Jimmy's new tract on the Nett River. In that interim he made uncounted forays into the forests of Michigan and Wisconsin but did not find Tiwanah or even a trace of her tribe. By the time he got to the Nett, Paul was again working as a faller. He brought Babe along, but not as a work animal, actually giving up a day's wages each week in return for barn space and hay. Jimmy Knox accepted that arrangement, and Paul seemed restored to something of his old self.

He moved into the bunkhouse with the cutting crew. He played checkers and listened to the boys' endless bullshit. Most of all he returned to work on the spring boards with the two-man saw and the axe, and everyone agreed there was not a logger anywhere could fell timber like the red-bearded demiurge from Round River.

It was sometime in mid-May that Paul ran across Swede Sturleson's men. Jimmy's cutting crew had already quit camp and Paul was not interested in driving logs down the Nett. He had other ideas for the summer ahead. But Paul needed a place to barn Babe, so Jimmy let him abide through the solstice at Camp Two in return for odd jobs around the site. He might reshingle the shantyhouse roof or rehinge a barn door.

Sometimes Jimmy would send Paul out to bring in equipment or supplies for the coming year. Then there was this one occasion Paul was enlisted to deliver a corpse.

One of Jimmy's men died his first week riding sticks, but the circumstance, so far as river drivers judged such things, was desultory. Far from being crushed to death between timbers or dismembered through a sluice, the young man apparently died of pneumonia, a consequence of mere days soaked to the bone in chilling water and spray.

The deceased came from a large family who insisted on burial in the family plot, so Jimmy had Paul hitch a wagon and told him to transport the body to a railhead at the company warehouse miles away. Paul loaded the corpse by himself, wrapping the remains in a tarpaulin between blocks of ice as Jimmy peeled off a wad to pay the freight.

"All you need to do is make the delivery and get a receipt," Jimmy told his summer hire. "Be damn sure you get the papers signed off. Last thing in the world I want is to have some lawyer suing me for failure to turn over a dead man."

This was a Sunday. The company warehouse was situated on the Ontonagon branch of the Saint Paul road and by the time Paul arrived the night train was long gone. There wouldn't be another feeder until ten o'clock the next morning which meant that Paul had to contemplate spending the night with a body on a bed of melting ice. Fortunately, the company warehouse was equipped to solve that problem. The company stocked all sorts of supplies at its depot, including perishables, which required a large walk-in icebox. There was a guard hired to keep security at night, so of course that fella was sound asleep until

Paul nudged his chair with his boot.

"Jesus!"

The poor bastard woke up to see a logger seven feet tall with a corpse over his shoulder.

"Jesus and Mary!!"

"It's fine," Paul assured the company man. "He's only staying the night."

With the stiff resting easy in the company cooler and the guard mollified with a George Washington, Paul turned his attention to his animals. Once the horses were loosed from their traces, watered, and stabled, Paul made sure they got a bag of oats each. Only then did he begin to consider how to manage his own affairs for the night.

He'd worked up a thirst along with an appetite on the road and was wondering if the clerk could be persuaded to loan him some victuals from the company's ice chest when a commotion from the warehouse's office got his attention.

The office itself was a separate structure situated directly opposite the loading dock, a box of pine planks and cedar shingles sheltering an open bay of desks and countertops that looked through upraised windows across the narrow porch to the dock and rail lines beyond. The bean counters were gone for the weekend, but a group of lumberjacks had missed their train and appropriated the space. Paul could see a demijohn passing from one hand to the 'nother in the glow of kerosene lanterns inside.

Judging by the jug's easy dip, they'd been at it awhile. Paul strolled up to the verandah and on his approach began to make out snatches of inebriated conversation.

"… you see that thang burn?"

"God O Mighty."

"Them… horses…!"

Paul paused at the door. It wasn't hard to eavesdrop on a bevy of lumberjacks primed with moonshine. There were five of them, or at least that's what Paul could make out from his vantage on the porch.

River drivers, from the look of 'em. Overalls and spiked shoes. Paul could hear them bragging all the way out on the porch.

"… Somebody tole me Jimmy's still blamin' the redskins!" One of the drivers chortled derision.

"… Got nobody to blame but hisself," another replied. "Mr. Sturleson made him an offer. He should of took it. Ain't that right, Larki?"

Larki Jay?!

Paul dropped to a knee to risk a sustained view through a window near the door. Yep, there was the timber agent. His back was turned to the door, but you couldn't mistake the small dark frame and that goddamn hat.

"What about it Mr. Jay?" One of the hogs, a big fucker with a face ravaged by smallpox challenged the little Finn. "Is it Jimmy's fault or our'n?"

Larki spread his hands.

"Boys, I ain't your boss."

"Got that right."

"But if Mr. Sturleson told you to burn the barn, seems to me that's his responsibility."

"Well, now," another voice chimed in from a tall, raw-boned logger.

Paul recognized the voice before he spotted the long ponytail run through a loop of cowhide. A run of blond hair streaked now with gray. The last time Paul had seen Hel Helson was a hundred or so feet off the ground in unfriendly competition. Their only physical contact involved a plank ripped from a privy. Clearly, nothing in the intervening years had curbed Hel's thrall to The Swede.

"Boss says you put a match, you put a match."

Helson offering this pearl as though he were Kierkegaard.

"If Jimmy Knox had shit for brains he'd of taken the damn money an' he'd still have his barn and his horses both."

The poxed logger seemed intrigued by that line of thought.

"I don't think you boys have anything to worry about, in any case," Larki interposed. "There's nothing connecting you to the barn, much less the livestock. The evidence, as they say, is gone up in smoke."

"'In smoke'! You hear that, boys?!"

Hel belching laughter with the rest. Meaty hands slapping thick-set thighs.

Larki Jay poised like a parakeet between them.

That's when Paul decided, as they say, to join the conversation and, raising a size-twenty boot, kicked the door off its hinges.

"THE FUCK?"

The jug shattered on the floor as The Swede's men dived for cover or weapons. The driver nearest Larki came at Paul with a bowie knife. Paul turned that blade aside and broke the man's arm, and he goes down screaming curses. That left four more to tangle.

It was a melee. Nothing scientific. Paul was picking up everything he could snatch to break over somebody's head. He had the advantage of surprise and he was an Ajax in his prime, but these were The Swede's men, hard and used to violence, and numb with alcohol. And these were men bringing knives and pikes where Paul brought fists and furniture.

Paul got inside the swing of a peavey and turned that spike back to gut its owner. He head butted the next driver and took the graze of a blade in return. Two men left and these were men who knew what they were doing.

"Do I know you?" Helson demanded behind his knife.

"You should," Paul replied. "I was a regular headache."

Helson crabbed sideways to flank Paul on one side as the man with the cratered face circled 'round with a cant hook.

"The shit *are* you?" Helson challenged once again.

"Remember Madawaska?" Paul picked up an oak-ribbed chair by the legs. "It's only been a decade. Or what about Beaver Lake?"

Helson paused.

"Well, I be damned. Piotir's whelp. The cow fucker."

"So you remember Babe then."

"I remember a outhouse, too, but you won't get that chance again."

Helson feinted a stab with his long knife. His mate charged with the cant hook from the other side.

Paul went straight over the cant to slam a ledge of maple straight through the man's neck and Crater Face went down on a floor slick with booze. That made four down out of five.

But it left Hel Helson free to attack from behind.

Larki Jay saw the blade go in, just below Paul's shoulder, Paul turning then with a grunt.

Just a grunt, Larki would later say. Like he was bit by a bee or some nuisance.

Paul turned and kicked Helson straight in the chest. The knife clattered to the floor.

"I want you to think about them horses," Paul said and dashed a burning lantern onto the floor.

The lamp's bowl shattered and kerosene spilled onto a floor already primed with moonshine.

A fire broke out with a whooooosh!

"YOU… FUCKER…!!"

Helson charged through rising flames, and Paul met him head-on, throwing his arms around his papa's killer in an awful embrace.

Jerking him off the floor.

"You bastard!"

Helson thrashed wildly, his pigtail slapping back and forth, but then Paul Bunyan gave a mighty shrug and it was like sticks breaking, ribs and spine snapping like dried kindling.

A scream gargled in Helson's throat, and then he went limp as a sock, a trail of piss and shit running down his trousers.

"Fuck me!" Helson cried, and Paul dropped him into a pool of his own defecation.

"My... my legs!" Helson bawled from the floor.

"I CAN'T FEEL MY FUCKING LEGS!"

The flames licking closer, now. Black smoke rolling.

"Jesus Christ!" Larki Jay made a break for the door, but Paul snatched him back.

"You."

"Don't! Please don't!"

The timber agent jerking like a chipmunk in Paul's hand.

"PLEASE!"

"Shut up," Paul said with a smile.

Heaving like an ox on a steep grade.

"What...?! What do—?!"

"What do I want, Mr. Jay? I want to break Swede Sturleson's goddamn neck. I want to watch the blood come out his eyes."

"I didn't know about Beaver Lake!" Larki begged. "I didn't

know anything!"

"Liar."

Paul tossed the timber agent out the door like a beanbag.

"Tell The Swede I'll be waiting."

"*YOU CAN'T LEAVE ME!*" Hel Helson screamed as Paul steps out to the porch.

"*YOU FUCKING FREAK!!*"

"Just think about the horses," Paul advised.

And left Hel to burn.

Chapter Seventeen
Exile and Exodous

By the time the train arrived at the Ontonagon warehouse Monday morning there were six sets of remains to be freighted out, only one of which was recognizable. The sheriff came in on the next train, but by then Larki Jay was gone and the guard was not able to tell the lawman much of any use.

"I smelled smoke, and I ran out of the warehouse to see the office on fire. Jimmy's man was there, the big redhead. He was holding himself kinda stiff, like he'd busted somethin'. 'I'll be takin' my team back' was all he said. Just like that. Like they weren't a fire blazin', nor anything else out of the ordinary.

"Anyways, I go runnin' toward the office, and there's Larki Jay on the dock, shaking like a leaf in the wind. 'He killed 'em,' I heard him say. 'He left 'em to burn.'"

By the time the authorities reached the timber agent, he was once again at Beef Slough. Facing a marshal and a Pinkerton agent, Mr. Jay denied saying anything to the warehouse guard the night that Sturleson's men were cremated.

"It was just a fire," Larki told the sheriff. "The boys were drinking and nodded off and there was a fire. That's all."

"What about the man from Jimmy Knox's camp? The big redhead. What was he doin' at the office?"

Larki shook his head. "Can't help you there."

The county sheriff up by Nett River got a judge to issue a subpoena to compel Paul's witness.

"What's the name on the warrant?" the clerk wanted to know, and several options were offered before a pay stub was produced for one *Paul Christian.*

Of course, it didn't matter. The writ was worthless unless it could be served, and no one had any idea where Paul could be found. Within weeks the authorities wrote off the deaths of Hel Helson and his 'jacks as an accident. The case was closed so far as The Law was concerned.

But Swede Sturleson had his own conversation with Larki Jay. He caught up with Larki in Alma, did The Swede. He took a hot poker and branded the Finn right on his face, and as Larki screamed, The Swede offered other persuasion.

"Tell me what happened, you little fuck, or the next poke's goin' up yer arse."

It's a sure bet Larki gave up everything he knew, but he couldn't tell Sturleson where to look for Paul because he didn't know where Paul was. None of us knew. Paul did return to Jimmy Knox's camp; that much was certain. Jimmy told the sheriff he'd got up early Monday morning and learned that Paul was cleared out.

"Got his gear out of the bunkhouse and skedaddled, what I can tell," Jimmy declared. "He brought my wagon and horses back. That and a receipt of payment for freighting a corpse. But after that Paul hit the skids, and he took Babe with him."

Paul had every reason to run. First off, even though he was

ostensibly subpoenaed as a witness, Paul wasn't about to trust any writ served by a lawman under a timber baron's thumb. Even had he been assured the law was not interested in him as a suspect for homicide, Paul knew better than to wait for Swede Sturleson's verdict in that question. Left to himself, the local sheriff might be content to accept the deaths of Hel and the others in Sturleson's crew as accidental, but The Swede, you could bet, would not.

It made sense to run to ground, and even Paul could disappear into the forests of Michigan's Upper Peninsula. These were deep woods ideal for a man lingering outside the reach of law or vengeance. That said, Paul told me he'd not planned to hide among natives. What he intended to do was to find a safe passage across the Lakes and back to Canada, back to his highland haunts.

But getting to Canada posed risks. Paul couldn't risk taking a public ferry or boat; he was just too easy to spot. Same thing for train travel. The Pinkertons were alerted to the slaughter on the Saint Paul Road and were not likely to let a red-bearded suspect the size of a small tree slip through their fingers. And then there was Babe. Even if Paul managed to escape notice, his ox would not.

It's difficult to go on the lam with a bull the size of a shed.

In any case, Paul didn't make it to Canada. He could not have made that journey even with clear sailing. He'd taken a knife that in a normal man would have gone right through the lung. Hel Helson did not get his blade to Paul's lung, but it was a dirty blade going through a shirt never cleaned and within hours the wound was inflamed.

Even we moderns are impotent in the face of sepsis or gangrene. A limb can be amputated, but a knife wound to the chest or abdomen is not amenable to that procedure. The best hope was to clean the wound quickly with carbolic acid. A good surgeon would then probe Paul's shoulder for flannel or other foreign debris with the potential to foment infection. That protocol has been followed in logging camps and on battlefields for the past century.

But Paul did not have a surgeon, not even a barber. He left the Nett River on Babe's broad back with a jug of cider, his father's rifle, and a bindle of clothes, following skid rows on a retreat to the deep forest where he collapsed delirious and moaning at a steaming spring on a creek running freely with the spring thaw.

Tiwanah found Paul where she first saw him. She would later admit to me that she was not initially so much interested in Paul as in Babe, an avatar recurring in dreams on both sides of the Gitchegoome.

"The bull has in him the Manitou," Tiwanah declared. "If I had found Paul-son alone at the Spring of Hot Rocks, I probably would have left him to meet the Great Spirit, but his totem was there, the bull, and I was loath to offend such magic."

Tiwanah made a travois for the wounded man and hitching that drag to Babe transported Paul deep into the forest and safe haven with her band of Potawatomi.

The tribe's medicine man had the women clean and cauterize the gash in Paul's back. He offered supplication. Then he ordered Paul moved to sweat out his fever in a wigwam hotter than a fresh-fucked fox in a forest fire.

When he came to, there was Tiwahah.

"Why am I here?"

"Your bull roams in my father's dreams," Tiwanah told him. "You wander."

But Paul would not wander again for a long time. He'd remain with Tiwanah for the rest of that year and for several years following. His status among the Indians derived from their reverence for Babe, even though the band benefited hugely from having a skilled woodsman in their debt. Paul built or repaired any number of rope bridges linking the village to trade routes and hunting grounds, and rebuilt the Potawatomis' longhouse.

Paul never claimed to be intimately familiar with the spirit life of his hosts, nor to understand their rituals. We immigrants from Europe or further abroad often speak knowledgeably of Indians and their Old Ways, but it's mostly nonsense. A bit like using a mirror to imagine what a fish sees.

Most of what we newcomers think we know about tribal life is the product of Wild West shows and dime novels. We imagine Custer fighting off hordes of marauding savages on horseback, but disease killed more Indians than the cavalry, and in any case by 1890 bands of Indians like Tiwanah's were largely pedestrian and passive.

But some remnants of tribal lore survive, even to modern times. Paul was surprised to learn that Tiwanah's people regarded trees as spirits, part of an all-encompassing Spirit, that could not be replaced. He was amazed at the power of dreams to shape daily decisions among tribesmen, and the deference paid to those gifted in their interpretation. Christians praying to God to heal their young or destroy their enemies should not feel superior.

But even though Paul was accepted in Tiwanah's hidden village, and even valued there, he did not fully understand her people nor did he expect them to understand him. Taking another example, it's romantic to imagine that Paul's ardor for Tiwanah was reciprocated. She gave herself to him easily. They were pregnant within months.

I once asked Tiwanah what it meant to be intimate with a man so different from her and her tribe.

"What you mean?"

"Well, how do you feel about him, I guess? As husband and wife?"

"Our husbands are usually chosen for us," she shrugged. "It is for our tribe. It brings good dreams."

We spoke for just a few minutes, but I gleaned from that exchange that Paul's was essentially an arranged marriage. Her father and the elders of her camp concluded that Tiwanah did not happen upon Paul and his sacred bull by accident. There had to be some design behind that unlikely circumstance, some purpose to be fulfilled. A marriage seemed prudent.

This didn't mean that Tiwanah resented her situation. On the contrary, she was very proud to be known as the wife of the man who brought the Great Bull totem to her village. And I am reasonably sure that Tiwanah appreciated Paul's affections. He was considerate, if a tad erratic in attention.

Paul definitely had an instinct for the dramatic that was greatly appreciated by natives and whites alike. I never will forget the flair with which our prodigal logger ended his self-imposed exile. In the years of Paul's absence, Crosshaul and Jean Lafayette had moved camps too many times to count, taking stumpage from Wisconsin to Minnesota before coming to Michigan. This'd be around the turn of the century, 1900 or so. We were set up in the Upper Peninsula on Onion River. It was a Sunday, right after supper. We'd just piled out of the cook house in a light snow when out of the gloom and through veils of gently blowing flakes of crystal we saw something moving just inside the tree line.

"The fuck is that?" Crosshaul asked.

Out came Paul and beside him an Indian woman we'd never seen. She was mounted on Babe's neck like some kind of Brahmin princess. It was Tiwanah. She had a blanket trimmed with fox-fur thrown over buckskin and beads, those long legs straddling Babe like a yoke.

We all 'bout dropped our drawers.

"Evenin', Boss," Paul called out to Crosshaul with a smile. "Any chance I can hire on?"

Well, that was a celebration. He was back! Out of the wilderness! Our prodigal son was returned, and no longer a kid, either. Paul was a man now.

A man with a wife.

"Knock me down with a fuckin' feather," Red Murphy swore.

Paul went out with Dirty Dan the next morning to team up on a cross-saw. Babe was handy to run lines back and forth between the donkeys, as docile as any mare. Jean Lafayette asked

Sourdough if he could use Tiwanah in the cook house, and that's how we wound up with a woman in camp. She was a great hand, too. Sourdough said if Paul didn't treat her right he'd marry her hisself.

Paul threw up a lean-to next to the barn for him and Teeny, as the men dubbed her, but he made a point every night to spend time in the bunkhouse with the fellas, and I have to tell you, that's where I think the tall tales really took off. The rookies, in particular, were already primed with stories about Paul and Babe. They couldn't get enough of him.

"Tell us everything," some newly hired logger would beg. "Tell us how you whupped The Swede's men. Or what about that time Babe pulled the river straight?"

All that was harmless enough. But then some crumb-boss yells out—

"What about Beaver Lake?"

You could hear a pin drop, and I thought, oh, shit, but Paul seemed prepared for the question.

"Well, it really didn't have nothing to do with me." Paul sucked on his pipe. "Nor with Babe, neither, or at least not principally."

"No?" The new kid was incredulous. "I heard you busted the dam and drained the lake, and then you and Babe snagged a brail of timber goin' over the spillway."

"Oh, they was plenty goin' downriver, but it weren't logs," Paul chided and then with a wink to us veterans. "Y'see Sourdough, he'd got so many men in camp that winter he couldn't feed us all at once. Couldn't find a skillet big enough, was the problem. But one day Sam's up by Beaver Lake, and he says to himself, 'Why, this is about right,' and then he sends for Babe to bring up a dozen boxcars' worth of lard and takes about half of a round forty of good white pine to get himself a fire goin', and first thing you know there's pancakes comin' up brown as a berry and light as goose down all the way from one side of Beaver Lake to the other.

"Course, Sam weren't thinkin' too clearly about the ice. So just about the time he had us all sat down and ready to pan those cakes, why, that's when the ice finally give way and the dam broke and every goddamn one of those johnnycakes went over the slip. To this day when you're on the Mississippi and you see them three and four-tiered paddle boats and gambling boats and barges steering around them islands, why, them ain't islands at all. They's what's left of Sourdough Sam's pancakes lost at Beaver Lake."

The new hires cheered that invention. We veterans breathed a sigh of relief. I didn't know what to think 'til Paul leaned over. "Now, Johnny," he said—

"That there is what you call an exaggeration."

It wasn't long before loggers from Ottawa to Portland were ginning up stories on their own to build a growing lore of adventure and predicament that involved Sourdough and Dutch and Red and all the rest of us in outlandish exploits with Paul and Babe, each tale more embellished and impossible than the one preceding. It was great fun for all of us, and Paul didn't mind.

He was back. He would kick up his heels when Red took the fiddle and buck dance with Big Ole. He'd cuss a blue streak over a checkerboard with Dirty Dan while he whittled himself a pipe from a cob of corn. There'd be letters read and written and socks darned and then the lanterns would sputter and he'd kind of stretch and say—

"Well, boys, I got a little woman waitin'. And a bundle in the oven, too."

Tiwanah was pregnant, Paul told us proudly, and Red Murphy made him drink a hogshead of beer.

There were congratulations all around, and then Crosshaul says, "Well, boys it's got to end sometime," and we all started looking for our racks.

"Don't miss the breakfast bell, Paul," Jean Lafayette sang out.

"Ne craignez rien." Paul grinned happily.

He bent 'bout double to squeeze out the door, and when he was gone everything went quiet.

"A baby!" somebody said finally. "Hot damn."

You could hear the woodstove clinking at the rivets. A sough of wind through the pines outside. Then Curly spoke up to comment about a baseball game or somebody's girlfriend and by lights out we were once again the best goddamned lumberjacks living and Paul was our bull of bulls. In that moment, you could almost forget that anything of importance ever occurred at Beaver Lake or the Ontonagon crossroad.

But Paul did not forget.

And neither would Swede Sturleson.

Sturleson had tracts up and down the Chippewa and was

expanding monthly, seemed like, to garner stumpage along the major trunks of rail. That put The Swede's men in lots of places, but logging camps in those days were isolated so as long as Paul stayed in camp under the eyes of his friends, there wasn't much chance he'd run into more trouble.

The long winter ended, and Jean released the cutting crew. This was around the first week in May, so we had about two weeks, little over, between cutting and driving. Paul had every intent to drive the river that spring; he actually looked forward to it. However, a telegram from Ottawa changed those plans. Paul's mama was not expected to live through the month. Elina was more than ninety years old and much too frail to leave her nursing home. If Paul was going to see his mama before she died, he'd have to risk a trip outside the safety of the Peninsula.

Paul chewed over the logistics and risks with me and Crosshaul and Jean Lafayette. We finally agreed that the best bet would be to follow the backways to Lake Huron, from there to catch a freighter or barge bound for the Canadian shore.

"Ottawa's safer for you now than Michigan," Jean advised Paul.

"I can't take Babe."

"Don't worry about your bull," Crosshaul admonished. "We'll take care of Babe. But I'm thinking it'd be a good idea to have somebody from camp go with you."

"Everybody's gone except the river drivers, and you sure as hell can't spare one of them," Paul cautioned.

Jean Lafayette glanced over to me.

"Johnny can go."

Paul smiled at me—a diminutive bookkeeper with a tonsure of hair and bifocals.

"I reckon you'd strike fear in most any assassin, Johnny."

"I can be nervous on your behalf at least," I tried to reply bravely, though in truth I would have passed this cup in a heartbeat if I could've figured out a way to do it.

So anyways, next morning Jean took us to a narrow-gauge railroad, and we rode a speeder all day to reach Lake Huron. The ferry had already run, so we paid a bosun on a coal barge to take us over to the Canadian side. Ten dollars to sit on top of a pile of lignite in a cold spring rain.

"At least we ain't attractin' attention," Paul said as sheets of sleet swept over the barge.

"I feel better already." I sneezed.

We spent a couple of miserable hours on that barge, and in that time Paul did something I can't remember him ever doing. He asked me about my name.

That wasn't the first thing he asked; Paul was more indirect in his approach, which of itself was uncharacteristic. He started by asking me what I did before scaling logs and counting beans in logging camps.

"Oh, nothing much," I evaded. "Worked in Cleveland for a while. Chicago."

"They fell trees in Chicago?"

"I was a junior employee in an investment firm," I told him. "We traded commodities, mostly. Wheat and corn. Pork bellies. Minerals, too, of course. Copper, especially. Some gold."

"Make any money?"

"For somebody, anyway." I nodded. "That's what got me in trouble."

"Aha," Paul replied, as if he already had the particulars.

"I didn't start out a thief," I insisted defensively. "At first I was just doing what my boss told me. 'It's a service fee,' the old man would say. 'Just something off the top for the firm.'

"Of course, every time I finessed the books to cover one of those transactions I'd come back to my cherrywood desk and there'd be an envelope with a sheaf of green inside. Once I got a salad for five hundred dollars. Always cash, never anything with a signature.

"It didn't happen all the time, just now and then. And I probably could have got away with it forever, if I'd kept my hands off the old man's daughter-in-law."

"Daughter-in-law? You tellin' me you cuckolded the boss's son, Johnny!"

"The boss's only son," I admitted. "Her name was Jane, and like me, she was plain and wanted attention. Had to want it pretty bad, I guess you could say, to spend time with me. It wasn't much, a few furtive nights, but her husband found out."

"Did he call you out?"

"Oh, no. That'd be too public. What financier wants it bandied about that his neglected wife is sleeping with a bean counter? No, what Mr. E. B. Shroeder, Jr. did was turn over my books to an auditor."

"Oh, shit."

"Oh, shit is right. The only reason I'm not in jail is because Mrs. Shroeder warned me. I took my wad, my glasses, and a train ticket and headed for the woods. Been scaling logs and making payrolls ever since."

Paul mulled that over a moment.

"Your name—it's not Inkslinger, is it, Johnny?"

I smiled bravely.

"It is now."

By the time we got to Ottawa the sun was out. It was one of those glorious spring days when black-eyed Susans and day-lilies popped out in flowerbeds and parks, and the sunlight filtered green through blossoms of cherry trees and dogwood.

We took a hansom downtown where we got crossed up in directions. Paul had not seen Elina since her initial installment and had no idea how to find her residence. Course, we had an address and with the driver's help eventually pulled up next to a four-story bungalow on a residential street. There were maple trees all around and a magnificent American elm throwing shade over a wide verandah redolent with honeysuckle.

I waited in the cart for Paul's return. I didn't figure it'd be more than an hour or so. You can generally run out of conversation with an aged parent in an hour, was my judgment. But I was wrong.

Paul was back in less than fifteen minutes, bending under the front door's lintel on a beeline for our hansom.

"How's Elina?" I asked.

"She's gone," he said.

I remember being irritated.

"Well, I hope at least they gave you an address."

"Johnny, she's gone for good."

It was a peaceful death, Paul told me. The matron tending Elina had just set her up in a rocking chair on the verandah for some hot tea.

"She set down a pot with some sugar and milk, and Mama thanked her," Paul relayed the details to me. "Nurse comes back ten minutes later and she noticed the tea'd gone cold in the cup. When she got closer she realized Mama'd passed on."

Elina was buried in a plot Paul had paid for years earlier from the sale of the family Bible. He paid for her apartment and care out of his own earnings. In fact, he was paid up through July, and being a bean counter, I felt obliged to point out that a refund was due.

"Your mama's passed. You aren't obliged to shell out for another day."

Paul shook his head. "I told 'em to keep it. There's lots of people in that place needs help, not all of 'em old."

Well, it was his business, not mine. Even so, it seemed a damned shame to've come all that way and have nothing to show for it.

"What d'you want to do, Paul?"

"See her grave." He handed a scrap of paper to the driver. "Then get back to camp."

Elina's final rest took her to the Notre Dame Cemetery in Ottawa. Coming in along the river you could see the Roman influence everywhere. In close proximity were the Grey Sisters' Motherhouse and St. Joseph's College, and there was the Notre Dame Basilica, rising high in Gothic Revival, the twin spires making an easy landmark.

I had the driver linger at the Archbishop's Palace; Paul was interested in the construction of the place, taking a lumberjack's appreciation of the labor and skill involved. He'd never seen a mansard roof, and in fact I believe the Palace was among the first buildings in Ottawa to incorporate that feature in its construction.

We found Montreal Road and the cemetery around noon. Paul gave a nun invisible beneath a white wimple and black wool a lot number and section, and she walked us through an iron gate and on to Elina's plot, just a simple granite headstone lined with hundreds of others dedicated to the Noble Mother between grassy aisles lined by rows of maple and other hardwoods.

"You were a good son to provide for her," the sister offered that severe comfort.

"You don't mind I'd like to have some time by myself." Paul took a knee. "I won't be long."

The sister excused herself entirely. I found a bench at some remove, and as Paul kneeled at his mother's grave, I wondered if it helped him to know that Elina was steeped in the rituals of the Church and believed its promises. I was pretty sure Paul did not share his mama's faith, but that's only speculation on my part. I certainly never pressed for those answers and the only time I ever heard Paul allude to the metaphysical was when I asked what he thought about Tiwanah's pagan heritage.

"It makes about as much sense as ours," was all he said.

We left the cemetery and I suggested a ride along the river. The sun was still bright, and our driver mentioned a winter fair that I hoped would lift Paul's spirits. We found the grounds easily, just a series of tents and booths set up offering everything from jewelry to blown glass. Being so near the city, the fair attracted hangers-on and well-to-do in roughly equal numbers, the brogans of bargemen or tanners crossing paths with the bustle of ladies in crinoline and men in ties and frock coats.

"Reminds me of Madawaska. Except with money," Paul recalled his first experience at a fair, which proved prescient.

There were outside talkers urging rubes into sideshows up and down a long midway. You could see the Fat Lady or Dog Man for a nickel. More innocent diversions took place in stalls or booths in open air. Here is where families crowded to toss rings around the necks of bottles or pepper a chain of metal ducks with a small caliber rifle. Paul ignored all of those diversions.

But right about the center of the midway a bally was getting started that caught Paul's eye. A talker replete in top-hat and striped trousers was stoking the crowd as two pairs of men shed their coats and ties to take opposite sides of a two-man cross-saw. A pair of logs presented the obvious challenge, their twin butts propped waist high on a heavily built sawhorse.

These contestants weren't experienced loggers. That much was obvious. But the talker was making hay with the locals, going on and on about the perils of the logger's life and the adventure to be had under the white pines of North America.

"These logs are a moment's work for the experienced

lumberjack." The host showed a mash of teeth through his handlebar moustache. "But you can experience the challenge yourself, man and boy. Just step forward and take a number. You can saw; you can wager; or you can saw and wager. First team cuts through his log wins."

It was a pitiful demonstration. A cross-cut saw is not something you can pick up like a fork and know how to use it, and a two-man bow requires as much finesse as a fiddle. What happened, predictably, was that gentlemen hoping to impress their ladies soon became objects of ribald comedy.

"Per yer back in it, gov!" a scruffy workingman ridiculed a well-suited contestant. In an admirable effort to double his effort the gentleman lost his footing and fell on his well-padded ass.

"Forfeit!" some bargeman cried out, and laughter exploded in about equal parts with argument, half the spectators howling derision while those with money on the line disputed criteria for disqualification.

Paul turned to me.

"You ever been on a saw, Johnny?"

"You know damn well I haven't."

"'Bout time, don't you think?"

"I do not."

"Come on, John. Let's show the gents how to make this whippoorwill sing."

Well, you can imagine the reaction of the crowd when Paul stepped over the ropes to approach the talker.

"Got you a new team." He tossed the man a coin. "Me and the inkslinger against whoever you got."

"That's a lopsided challenge if ever I saw one," the talker punned, and the crowd jeered.

Paul shrugged.

"Any team you like."

"I'll take that wager." A graveled voice rose from the other side of the ropes and a pair of honest-to-God loggers stepped from the crowd. They probably had been driving the river, these two. Taken a walk to blow their pay. The one fella was lean and strong; his partner was a little on the soft side, but nearly as tall as Paul. You wouldn't need to see the red flannel shirts and stagged trousers to know where they came from.

"I'm Forty Jones," the big man said. "This here is Jim Liverpool. We call him Long-Jump, which if you'd like to try him later, yer welcome. And who are you lot?"

"I'm, uh… I'm Johnny Inkslinger," I answered with some reluctance.

"Where you boys from?"

"The States," I equivocated. "Down Michigan way."

"And you, mister?" the talker turned to Paul. "We don't see many specimens like you, even on the midway."

Paul stalled a moment.

"…What's the name of this place?" he asked finally.

"Bunyan's Green," the front man answered.

"Fine." Paul nodded shortly. "Then I'm Paul Bunyan."

The talker chuckled.

"Fair enough. So Mr. Bunyan, do you accept the challenge of these fine lads here?"

"I tell you what," Paul replied. "I'll match these two 'jacks right by myself."

"*There's a wager!*" our host shouted joyfully and within seconds citizens of Ottawa were swapping bets like it was a racetrack.

Forty Jones and Long-Jump set up on the butt of their log, each man at opposed ends of a tuttle-toothed saw. Paul settled the teeth of his long blade carefully.

"Ready, gents? *Have at it!*"

Back and forth the saws sang, but never rushed. Back 'n forth, back'n'forth! Forty Jones and Jim had as many hours on a cross-saw as anybody, and they were damn good. You could see the easy rhythm, sawdust spilling to the ground with each pull. That distinctive lullaby of blade on wood.

But Paul was better.

I never would have guessed a single man could keep a saw built for two men in play, but he did. Each pull took the full length of the blade, and it never bound up, never stopped. In less than a minute's time Paul's butt end dropped to the ground.

"*WINNER IS MR. BUNYAN!*" the talker beamed, and even folks losing their wager had to admit it was entertaining to see. People cheered and clapped and threw coins to the barker in appreciation for the demonstration. I heard a loud plunk and be damned if somebody hadn't thrown our bally a silver dollar.

"Don't miss this one," I said and handed it over.

"Much obliged." He nodded gratefully.

A dollar in silver was worth something in those days. Even so, had I known where it came from, I'd have chunked that buckaroo into the river. I did not see the man who threw that geld, but if I had, I'd have described the gentleman as a large-framed man with big hands nearing sixty years old.

It was spring, so he might not have been wearing the distinctive bearskin coat, but you can be sure he was carrying a sidearm, and if you were very observant, you'd notice that the ring of minted silver prominently ornamenting The Swede's flat-brimmed hat was short by a silver dollar.

Chapter Eighteen
A Jam Of Logs

One of the things about Paul that used to perplex me was his obdurate refusal to see any manifestation of evil that was not personal. He watched me pay Larki Jay three hundred dollars in cash, for example, without realizing or acknowledging that it was an out and out bribe. Even before his wilderness days, when he was partnered with Crosshaul and Jean at the Round River camp, Paul refused to go over contracts or financial obligations shaded in gray.

I guess you could excuse that lapse by saying that Paul simply had a very selective intelligence. At work in the deep woods he was preternaturally alert. No detail of the environment escaped Paul's attention. A chick couldn't ride a loon's back unnoticed. Everything from a Hungerford's beetle to a black bear claimed his interest, and nobody was more alert around slip-tongues or donkey engines or livestock than our bull of the woods. He was like a damn owl, head always swiveling.

Taking everything in.

But when it came to the business end of things, Paul was worthless. It was a good thing he'd thrown in his share of the operation to Crosshaul and Jean; anyone else would have robbed him blind. One reason the boys liked playing cards with Paul was that he was so easy to cheat. Dan could deal the same ace off the bottom five times in a row and I doubt Paul'd notice.

Good thing they were playing for matchsticks.

By the turn of the century the timber business had become a high-stakes game, a casino for graft and corruption. The McKinley administration encouraged the ongoing transition from publicly owned land to private acquisition, and timber barons and railroad moguls happily gutted public resources for profit.

In that respect, Swede Sturleson was no worse than a thousand others. The Swede stood in the company of many barons who bought stumpage from the government at greatly deflated value, culled the timber, and then re-sold the land for big money down the line. Indians used to own enormous tracts of timber; they were among the first to be swindled. Independent operators, like our crew, were swallowed up next. And ordinary loggers happily abetted the big boys' schemes.

One of our own crew got caught up in one of The Swede's swindles. The fraud took advantage of a homestead law designed to encourage settlement and improvement of a squatter's land. Sturleson established a front company that paid any lumberjack thirty dollars a month and free board to homestead a quarter of a section of timberland for five years. After five years the logger was obliged to deed over his homestead to the logging company.

Government agents were supposed to inspect homesteaded tracts to make sure they complied with legal requirements, but all a man had to do was construct a dwelling for permanent residence having two windows. I've seen lumberjacks throw up a shanty in a day and stick in whiskey bottles for windows and the examining agent signed off without a qualm—in return for "consideration."

These and a hundred other shenanigans went on continually, but Paul never paid attention. In Paul's reckoning, Swede Sturleson was not a bad man because he stole land or defrauded the government. Sturleson was a bad man because he'd wronged Paul and his father personally with a result of injury and death. That's the sort of evil Paul recognized, that he understood, and that is the evil he would meet face to face.

It was a spring morning barely a week after I stood with Paul at his mother's grave that I looked up from a stack of contracts to find Swede Sturleson filling my door. There he was, dressed like a gentleman in fly-front trousers, a high-collared shirt and four-in-hand tie. I could see a pearl-handled revolver peeking from behind the folds of a fur-lined overcoat.

"Inkslinger."

"Mr. Sturleson."

He entered without permission, gathering a chair on the way as though it was his own.

"Make yourself comfortable," I drolled as casually as I could.

He took off his black hat, and I noticed there was a dollar missing from the sideband.

"Where's Paul?" he inquired.

"Paul who?" I asked, and he chuckled.

"I saw you in Ottawa, Johnny. You and Paul. I even made a little money on the side."

"The cutting crew's already hoofed, Mr. Sturleson. Paul could be most anywhere."

"I doubt it."

The Swede knew we were getting ready to drive our logs downriver, and he knew as well as I did that although the cutting crew had already left camp, Paul remained with his fellow river hogs to get our dams and sluices in shape for the coming frenzy.

"I hear you boys're havin' yerself a good year."

"Fair to middlin'," I fenced, not knowing exactly the extent of the baron's intelligence.

In fact, our camp felled something like four million feet of timber that year and with contracts already in hand figured to have our best season ever.

Sturleson fished a watch from his vest pocket to check the time.

"I hear you're pushing the Steuben Camp's logs for'em," he remarked absently.

"That's true," I allowed. "Fact, I was goin' over the contract when you admitted yourself to my office."

"'Office'!" he chortled and pocketed the watch. "That's rich. What's he payin' you?"

"None of your goddamn business."

I was getting nervous. Why the devil would Sturleson be concerned with our logs or Steuben's? It was very common for two or more logging companies to find themselves sharing a river or tributary. Sometimes smaller operators would try to piggyback on the big boys, but more commonly the begging operator would simply pay to have his own sticks pushed downriver by the larger operator's drivers. Two dollars a thousand was a fairly standard rate; of course, you had to scale the logs on the ice to make sure you weren't getting shortchanged.

Not that I'd ever had a problem with Mr. Steuben. In fact, I'd just inked a contract to take on his logs for the river drive. This'd be right at three hundred thousand board feet of white pine already boomed up with our own sticks at a lake heading the east branch of the Onion River. Paul and Dutch had worked hard the previous night to secure the logs inside boom-logs lined by half-inch test chains. I wasn't expecting any problems.

That is, until The Swede walked in.

"What do you want, Sturleson?"

"Got a proposition."

"Kind of proposition?"

"It's for Paul. An accommodation really. Or contract, if you like."

"I handle all contracts," I replied pointedly.

He shook his head.

"Not this one. See I got my own dams down along the Onion and before a single fucking stick from this camp goes through, Paul and me are going to need to even some scores."

"You even scores with Paul, you're likely to wind up in a box."

"We'll see about that."

"I'll call the sheriff, Sturleson, goddamned if I won't."

"Sheriff Foster? Call him. Fact, tell Hank I told you to call.

The fuck, Johnny, you think I'd come out here without takin' care of that little nuisance?"

I leaned back.

"The rivers are free, Sturleson. The hell makes you think you own them?"

"I'm just helping a few of the locals drive their logs." Sturleson opened his arms wide. "But I don't take kindly to piggybacks."

"Is that what you're worried about? We'll pay."

"You'll pay, all right."

"What's fair? Dollar-fifty? Two dollars a thousand?"

The Swede shook his head.

"My terms is with Paul and Paul alone."

"He won't meet you," I predicted.

"Then you can kiss yer cut good-bye, and Steuben's. I got men with rifles on every dam and sluice from here to Wisconsin. You won't get a single stick to the mill 'less I say so, not a goddamn straw."

"I'll wire the federal marshal, Sturleson. I'll send to the fucking governor if I have to."

"You do that. Meantime, stick your nose outside and you might notice the ice is melting. Three, four days at most the headwaters are gonna start pilin' up, and they ain't gonna stay forever. Another week and you'll have yerself a million feet of sticks stranded high and dry, so unless you think you can move the halls of government in seven days, you're gonna have to deal with *ME.*"

He shoved up from his chair and kicked it aside.

I hid my trembling hands in my lap.

"You tell Paul to meet me this coming Wednesday mornin'," Sturleson snarled. "Ten o'clock sharp. I'll be at the rollway just down from the west-branch dam. Tell him to come alone. I see any of you sons of bitches in escort the deal is off, you hear me? Well, do you goddamn hear me, Johnny?"

"I hear you."

"I'll let you know, then, what I want for yer logs. An' you can tell the redhead I'll keep it simple. I know he ain't got a head for figures."

That night I ran the boys out of the cook house to convene with Chris Crosshaul, Jean Lafayette, and Paul.

"I don't like it." Jean shook his head. "'Accommodation'? What does this mean?"

"Pretty fucking obvious it ain't about a contract," Crosshaul retorted. "Paul killed his best man, and then some, and The Swede means to settle the score."

"Why not just shoot me then?" Paul asked. "I'm out in the woods every day. He could have somebody ambush me there, or just wait till I'm coming back to camp."

"How do you know that's not what he intends?" I asked. "How do you know you're not walking into a bushwhack?"

About that time we heard a knock at the door. Now, that's something you just never hear, a knock on the door of a cook house at a logging camp.

In fact, at first we thought it was something kicked up in the wind rapping at the stalwarts.

But there it came again. A single knock this time. One rap of the knuckles.

"See who it is," Jean Lafayette said and I saw him pull a Derringer from his boot.

Crosshaul shoved off the deacon seat and approached the door to one side.

"Who is it?"

"*Frank Whitefeather*" came the muffled reply and we all stood as Chris opened the door for the gap tender from Beef Slough.

He was soaking wet the first time we'd seen him. He was half-starved now. Eyes sunk deeply into their sockets. Cheeks pulled in like an old man sucking a pipe.

"Why are you here?" Paul asked him.

"I—I had a dream," he croaked.

"Fucking Injun!" Crosshaul moved to throw the tender out on his ass, but Paul stopped the boss with one hand.

"No," he said. "Let him in."

With undisguised skepticism, Crosshaul relented. Jean Lafayette wasn't as accommodating.

"I don't trust bow-benders."

But Paul seated Whitefeather courteously. He offered some pork from the table. A biscuit.

Frank declined.

"But I take some beer, you have it."

I obliged with a jar of home brew which the Indian drained in a single pull.

"Haiee. That was good."

Paul leaned forward.

"Now, what did you see, Frank? What do you know?"

"I know the Great Spirit when I hear Him," Whitefeather answered and went on to recount his terrible dream.

This was late Friday. The wind picked up over the weekend and the first headwaters started piling up behind the dams. Paul went about his work as usual, except for adding Frank to the payroll.

"He's only hired for the day," Paul told me.

"And what day is that?"

"Wednesday."

Paul had already admonished the bosses and me to keep our consultation with Whitefeather confidential. He had a plan, Paul told us, by which we inferred some course of action predicated on the dreams of an inebriated Indian. And despite our pleas, Paul wouldn't share details, not with me or Jean or Chris.

"The Swede might have ears in camp, for all I know. And, anyway, what I got in mind you can't be part of."

"At least let a couple of the boys watch the rollway," I implored. "You can't see Sturleson right by yourself!"

"That's the only way he's gonna let me see him." Paul

contradicted me with a wan smile.

That weekend Paul packed up Tiwanah and sent her back to her people. He sent Babe along, too, a totem returned for safekeeping to Tiwanah's tribe.

"We take care of him," Tiwanah assured her husband.

Frank Whitehead accompanied Tiwanah and Babe to her village and Sunday's dusk came with a pall. The boys knew Paul wouldn't be sending away his wife and ox on a whim. The bunkhouse was quiet but for the whistle of a tea kettle and the slap of cards.

"You wanna tell us what the hell is goin' on?" Red Murphy asked Paul finally.

"When the time comes, you'll know," Paul answered, refusing to give any details of his intentions or any hint of Whitefeather's premonition.

Monday crawled by like the Inquisition. Then Tuesday came with a terrible storm. I've seen my share of blows on the Lakes and deep woods, but this was a beaut. Gale-force winds shrieked through the trees. Then came the lightning, the whole sky lit with bolt after bolt with barely a pause. You could have read a gazette in that awful limning.

With the lightning came fire. Part of a lumberjack's life is spent dreading conflagration. A single spark can torch sections of timber, especially if the understory is brittle and dry, but we were well into spring weather. Generally the thaw of April to May limits the spread of forest fires, but the blaze that weekend did not seem much mollified by the damp, possibly due to the bellows of a nearly-constant wind.

The boys noted the fire's trajectory as they buttoned down our camp. No one needed to be told what it was like to have a fire crown overhead and even though that wasn't a likely occurrence, no one was taking chances. Big Ole rolled out barrels from the smithy that we threw on top of the bunkhouse and cook-shanty to fill with water. Dirty Dan hitched up the water-wagon normally used to ice skids and soaked the ground around our shanties and outbuildings.

You could see the flames crawling from ridge to ridge, patiently, like the hem of a witch's gown dragged along the ground. By late afternoon the wind died down, and everything in camp was dusted in films of ash and soot, a gauze of smoke lingering with the smell of wild onions. The sun edged to the horizon an angry ochre ball, and Tuesday went dark in a bloody dusk.

And all of that was foretold in Whitefeather's dream, along with the other.

The sun rose Wednesday with rings of fire coming to life in a new zephyr.

"Maybe Sturleson won't come." Crosshaul scanned the sky. "Maybe he'll wait for things to die down."

"Things are already died down so far as Sturleson's concerned," Paul replied, and then—

"Get the boys in the cook house. It's time they knew what's about."

Paul left camp with Frank Whitefeather early Wednesday morning. He hitched a wagon, a single mare traced to a bed lightly loaded. I asked Paul again what he intended.

"Just keep an ear out," was all he'd say.

The rollway specified for Paul's rendezvous with Swede Sturleson was half a mile downstream from the reservoir holding back a rising wall of water and four million feet of virgin pine that we'd labored all winter to fell and yard.

We couldn't break that dam so long as the sluices and dams downstream remained under Sturleson's control. Our logs were trapped in a rising pond of icy water, and we all wondered what sort of accommodation The Swede would demand to set those logs free.

Until Paul's recount, I was never sure of the details of the morning's powwow, but I did see what happened. I climbed a ridge with Crosshaul and Jean Lafayette on the bank opposite the rollway. We braved the fire to capture that perch, mute and helpless observers of the encounter below.

I should not have been surprised to see Paul find Sturleson's location from an unexpected avenue.

"I could see he had men with rifles on the bluffs above the rollway," Paul recalled the day. "There wasn't anybody on the east side, though, because of the fire, so it was natural for The Swede to have his men looking for me to come from the west bank of the river.

"But I didn't come from the east or the west. I put in at Twin Falls and came upstream."

The Swede was alerted with a rifle shot from the bluffs of Paul's approach. He'd come alone as directed, rowing against the current toward the dam in a shallow-drafting bateau.

"Ten o'clock sharp." Sturleson worried the fob at his vest as

Paul slipped oars.

"Heard you had a score to settle." Paul killed the boat's throw in the bank's soft sand.

"You heard right."

"Get in then." Paul nodded to a seat sternward. "We'll chew 'er over."

"Makes you think I'm interested in a boat ride?"

"I'm not going to linger in range of your rifles, Sturleson. I'm not a goddamn fool."

"That remains to be seen," The Swede leered, but stepped into the johnny.

The two men didn't have much to say as Paul pulled his flat bottom around and settled the oars in their locks for a short pull upstream.

"That should do it." He came about to drift a couple of hundred yards below the dam.

The Swede opening his overcoat to display the revolver.

"You could've shot me back yonder," Paul commented.

"Not till we parlay." The baron flashed yellow teeth. "I ain't forgot what you did to Helson and my boys."

"I haven't forgot what you did to me and my papa," Paul rejoined.

Sturleson spit carefully over the side.

"You're a pissant son of a bitch, ain't you? Cock of the walk? Bull of bulls?"

"I never claimed anything."

Sturleson barked a short laugh.

"Well, the stories will end today. I'm gonna shoot you in the gut, Mr. Bunyan, yes, I am. But not before I tell how I'm gonna ruin your camp, your crew, that goddamn Canuck Lafayette and Crosshaul and that little shit Inkslinger—I'm going to ruin 'em all."

Paul smiled.

"I take it you aren't here to negotiate a contract for pushing our logs downriver?"

"You take that right."

"What if Crosshaul offered you a part of our take?"

Sturleson sneered.

"I don't want his money. I want him broke on a wheel along with every son of a bitch ever worked with you in the woods. It's not just you I aim to take down, you redheaded freak. It's your crumbs, your whistle punk, your boss, your squaw, your fucking ox, when I find him, and I will. I want you to know before you die that everything you ever loved or touched is going to ruin at my hand."

Paul sighed.

"And do you 'spose I came here expecting differently?"

"I could give a rat's fuck what you expect." Sturleson released the leather loop trapping the hammer of his revolver.

Paul replied to the threat with an apparent non sequitur.

"Is that a Hamilton?"

"The fuck do you mean?" Sturleson hesitated over his sidearm.

"The watch on your fob there. Your vest pocket. That's a Hamilton, isn't it? Pretty good timepiece?"

"Never loses a minute."

"What I thought. And what time is it now?"

"'Bout a minute till I kill you."

"You might want to check the time first," Paul cautioned.

"And why's that?"

"Because at a quarter past ten o'clock sharp, I'm settling the score between us."

That's when the dynamite went off. Sturleson's head jerked upstream on instinct to see a dam's worth of water and mud thrown into the air with an entrée of rolling thunder. A cloud of debris and timber skyrocketing into a sky already heavy with ash, hanging like a thousand kites for just a moment, a moment only, plunging then into the river, tons of debris crashing into the Onion.

The dam bulged out from a ruptured seam. And then it busted wide open.

There would be no gradual relief of pressure from the headwaters that for days were piling behind the dam's earthen reservoir. There would be no careful release of water. These logs would not be sluiced in the waning breeze of moonlit labor. Paul had directed Frank Whitehead to blow the bottom out at fifteen minutes past the hour, and when the Indian's fuse reached the blasting cap—

The bottom of that dam got kicked out like a foot through a hatbox.

Boooooommmm!

The explosion echoed downriver. I felt the concussion on my skin half a mile up a ridge.

And there was Swede Sturleson trapped in a bateau with Paul Bunyan two hundred yards downstream with a tidal wave of timber bearing down.

"You son of a bitch!"

Paul shrugged.

"You crazy bastard!" Sturleson snarled and drew his revolver.

"Sure you wanna do that? Look upstream, Sturleson. See what's coming."

Sturleson swiveled to face the dam, and what he saw rising like a wall toward his fragile bateau was a tsunami of timber. Tens of thousands of logs spilling over the broken dam in headwaters running flat out.

"We got ten seconds." Paul spit a wad over the side. "Fifteen at most."

"Get us out of here! Get us ashore!"

"Can't make the shoreline." Paul shook his head. "The sticks're comin' too fast for that. We're gonna have to run with the timber."

"You son of a bitch, *GET US OUT OF HERE.*"

"Drop yer pistol over the side," Paul directed.

"Fuck you."

"Shoot me then. Or can't you manage a boat and paddle?"

By then a swell of water fifteen feet high was rolling toward the two men, a wave rising high as a barn. The Swede's men were scrambling like beetles on the bluffs above, a confusion of shouts and imprecations lost in the din.

Four seconds tick by. Five... Six...

"You think you can save us?" Paul smiled.

"*DAMN YOU!*" Sturleson screamed.

And threw his revolver at the coming tide.

Paul put his back into the oars, and the bateau practically leapt off the water. The first few logs had already caught up with that flimsy shell, two-ton timbers racing by like torpedoes with tens of thousands cresting high overhead.

A year of wood riding a wall of water.

"*PULL!*" The Swede yelled impotently. "*PULL, GODDAMN YOU!*"

The cresting wave overtook the bateau and tossed that bark into the air like a matchbox. The bateau fishtailed once, then plunged out of sight in a swell of mud and timber.

For seconds we couldn't see anything but foam and logs, tens of thousands of sticks seething bank to bank in a raging torrent. And the sound! You could hear the assault of water and timber, the concussion of log on log, the thunder of water and breaking ice. You could feel a breeze stirred up in the face of that oncoming fury.

"They're fucked!" Crosshaul gasped.

And I agreed. No matter how strong or skilled Paul was, he could not possibly move his flimsy skiff sideways against that torrent of timber. Paul's bateau had no more chance than a nutshell in a grinder.

But the shell survived that first plunging wave. The initial tsunami rolled over and be goddamned if the bateau did not pop up from the bowels of that river like a cork breaking through a cord of kindling, and there was Paul fending off a thirty-foot log with the butt of his paddle!

The Swede's knuckles white and brassless on the gunwales.

Hanging on for dear life.

"PULL!"

The old man screamed again and again against the roar of water and timber.

"PULL, DAMN YOU!"

Paul pulled them out of a peril and into a trap. A sea of logs now penned the bateau on all sides, timbers thick as a man is tall and thirty feet long closing about Paul's flimsy hull in a raging cataract.

Paul slipped an oar to stab a log as casually as if he were gigging a fish.

Then it was back to the locks, Paul looking for a hole, any hint of clear water in that sea of pine. And it looked like he'd made it, too. The initial tsunami was rolled past, and Paul had the bateau steady inside a gush of logs.

But then another hazard presented itself, and The Swede turned to follow Paul's eyes to the waterfall ahead.

"Jesus and Mary!" the old man swore.

Twin Falls was not a huge drop as waterfalls go, maybe twenty, twenty-five feet, but untold deals of logs were now racing for that spill. To make matters worse, the river narrows at the falls, forcing water and timber into a funnel maybe fifty yards wide, so the closer you get, the faster the water runs, and the timber, too.

Swede Sturleson could see white water boiling on all sides. He could hear the drone of the falls ahead, a basso profundo of water and timber thrown into an icy boil.

"*WE GOT TO PUSH FOR SHORE!*" The Swede bellowed.

Paul swayed to balance himself in a boat tossing like a cork in a teapot.

"You can try," he challenged. "There's always a chance."

"We can't go over the falls, you crazy fuck. We got *no* chance there!"

"I'd agree with that."

And as men watched from bluffs and banks on both sides of the bank, Paul slipped an oar and broke it over his knee.

"The fuck are you doing?" Sturleson exclaimed.

"I'm settling the score, Swede."

The bateau was now gaining speed in a race toward a deadly shelf. You could see death waiting in white sheets of water and mounds of foam angry on the lip of that spillway. You could see logs gone airborne to crash in a tangle below.

Paul tossed Sturleson the remaining oar.

"Your best bet is to keep 'er straight, get as much speed as you can and then hang on."

"Goddamn you, boy, if I get out of this—!"

"You're not gettin' out of anything, Sturleson. You wanted to take your time enjoying our little accommodation? Well, here she comes. Enjoy yourself."

With that encouragement, Paul abandoned his papa's killer, stepping as lightly as a bridesmaid from the bow of his flat bottom onto the back of a pressing log.

I'd give a lot to have seen Sturleson's face in that moment. Here was Paul digging his calks into one log after another in a desperate traverse for the shoreline while The Swede spins like a leaf in a gutter for the waterfall ahead.

The sound—! Like a freight train. Water and wood thrown together.

"Sturleson's a goner." Crosshaul crossed himself as he watched. "He's too close to the falls!"

But Paul was being pulled toward the shelf, too! He was doing his best to beat that deadly current, but the logs were sweeping for the falls, and taking Paul with them.

You've seen lumberjacks face off to birl a log? Two men contesting a stick secured in a gentle pond? Well, try that contest on a pile of timber moving faster than a dog can run in headwaters bound for a twenty-foot fall. It was like watching a Polynesian ride a surf mined with trees.

And we all realized in the same moment that Paul couldn't make it.

"He's too late!!" Jean cried. "*HE WAITED TOO LATE!*"

Paul was too close. The river was running too fast.

But there was a logjam.

More accurately, there was a stand of logs placed deliberately to ensure a jam. Paul had gone out with Frank Whitefeather the night before to plant a thicket of logs between a pair of granite boulders rising just upstream of the falls. These were boulders that had always caused us problems, a consistent site for jams.

"He's not headed for shore!" I shouted. "*LOOK BOYS!*"

The logjam was Paul's salvation, an island of pine piled against a backstop of solid granite. Paul timed a leap from a passing log onto that crag and clambered up its modest face as four million feet of logs swept by.

He stood there soaking wet but safe to see the bateau spinning toward the spillway ahead.

You could see Sturleson fighting the current up to the last moment, beating the water with his oar, stabbing at the crush of logs with that pitiful cant. The bateau splintered like a walnut just before the lip of the falls, and the last thing I saw as Sturleson went over was a wink of silver from the sideband of that goddamn hat.

His screams and curses were pillowed in the falls' relentless drum. Mr. Sturleson disappeared in a crush of timber and tumult, and in the moments following you could see his hired hands turning away one by one, those henchmen melting into a haze of smoke and sun like phantoms into a bank of dirty clouds.

By that afternoon, the rollways and dams were clear and

there were no rifles to block our drive downstream. The Swede's hired men turned their backs on their fallen boss and never looked back. Sturleson would be found days later, or rather parts of him, thrown up near the river's mouth. It took a while to identify the remains.

He was buried in Ottawa at the Notre Dame Cemetery in a fancy mausoleum directly across a yard of graves from Paul's foster mother. Was ironic, I suppose, that Swede Sturleson waited for Judgment a stone's throw from the wife of the man he murdered. The obituary in Ottawa ascribed the timber baron's death to accident. "… As have so many others, Thor Sturleson was crushed by the very logs that made him rich," the paper rambled and nobody cared enough to challenge that narrative.

Paul had no time for funerals. The day after The Swede met his fate, Paul was back on the river breaking jams and salvaging logs stranded in the deluge. By Friday we'd got that job done and had enough water at the dam below Twin Falls to sluice our logs on the next push down the Onion. By month's end we delivered our cut as contracted.

By June of 1901 it was over. You'd think there'd have been all sorts of stories passed on in the wake of that drive, the showdown with Sturleson, the fire and the logjam, and the rest, but as Jean Lafayette observed, it poisons the soul to celebrate the death of any man, even one as adamantine in enmity as The Swede. "Tales of vengeance are not tall tales," Jean insisted, and in any case there were practical reasons to want Sturleson's death recorded as the river's revenge and not Paul's.

Years later Big Ole asked me what I thought gave the kid the idea to risk putting himself in a boat with The Swede in front of a busted dam, and I told him about Whitefeather's dream.

"Frank said he saw the dam break. And then he said he saw a hat with silver dollars at the bottom of Twin Falls."

Big Ole snorted. "That's just Injun talk."

"Maybe," I allowed. "But Paul believed him. And Paul made it come true."

And that is not gilding the lily.

EPILOGUE

I WISH I COULD TELL YOU THERE IS A HAPPY-EVER-AFTER TO anticipate in the testament of Paul Christian Bunyan, but that would not be truthful. I'm not saying that in the years after Fence River, Paul didn't find occasions to enjoy the bunkhouse or fiddle. He did. But a logger's life is never easy. It was not until Paul's twilight years that camps accommodated families or long-term attachments. Logging was always for Paul Bunyan a peripatetic occupation.

He left the Upper Peninsula sometime around 1905 for the Pacific Northwest and I followed him. In the next fifteen years, the loggers we'd known and worked with retired or died. The war claimed a few. Long-Jump Liverpool leapt a twelve-foot trench bristling with bayonets only to land on a German mine. Tom McCann survived America's winter forests to be gassed one summer in the Ardennes.

They died but they were not forgotten, not all of them, anyway. By the time Paul reached the Cascades, Tom McCann and Shot Gunderson and Dutch Jake and Dirty Dan and Red Murphy were the stuff of lore, amalgams of fact and fable ginned up in shanty houses or in magazines published by timber companies looking to popularize their subscriptions. School teachers read children tales of Forty Jones and Jim Liverpool along with the antics of Sourdough Sam and Ole The Blacksmith.

By 1920 a logger could leave his work in the woods and be home in time to supper with the wife and kids, but Paul's wife did not make the journey west. The child she conceived was stillborn, which caused great consternation among the Potawatomi. Any child's passing was a serious matter, an omen requiring immediate interpretation, and an exanimate fetus might even represent a death knell for the tribe itself. The elders consulted with their shaman and decided that Tiwanah's mate had no further role to play in their dreams.

Paul took a few weeks that summer to settle his affairs. He did visit his wife one last time. Paul told me that her people treated him courteously, but there was no question of taking Tiwanah from her village. He received the tribe's decision, a kind of divorce I guess you could call it, with equanimity.

"She took me to the hot springs afterwards. We made love. She made a pillow for me, from her very own blanket, and when I woke she was gone."

Paul accepted all this with what I thought was either alarming alacrity or admirable stoicism. Or maybe he really wasn't cut out for married life. Oh, he'd have stayed in that hidden village forever, had the child come, I am sure of that. But with that promise gone, there was not a lot to claim Paul's attention in the Upper Peninsula. He followed the forest's siren westward.

And Babe?

Babe remained in the deep forest with Tiwanah's people. He was past his working years by then, but revered as a special gift of Gitchi Manitou. It wasn't easy for Paul to part with his daily companion. There was a symbiosis between Paul and Babe that was undeniable, some raw and primal force kindled between them. The Blue Ox was Paul's totem as much as the Indians'.

That said, Paul understood in a manner past my ken that in the eyes of the Potawatomi his bull ox had great potential to balance the death of his child. It was the sort of metaphysical calculation I find nonsensical, but no crazier I suppose than the rites intoned daily in sight of the twin spires in Ottawa.

We all die.

We all hope at some point for life beyond death.

I had Paul Bunyan's last will and testament ready for his signature sometime around May of '21. There were a few delays, some property in Ottawa of which I was unaware had to be added to Paul's modest assets, and I'd made a small investment in railroad stocks on Paul's behalf that he decided to cash in. It had taken many evenings of conversation, lots of tobacco, and one testy correspondence with the Bureau of Indian Affairs, but by January I was notarized as the executor of Paul's estate, and by the following May had an original and one copy of a will ready to be signed.

Paul took a speeder in from the woods to meet me at my office in the same nook where we'd been huddled for many, many evenings of collaboration. Winter's chill had given way to a balmy spring, but I still had a fire in my stove and a teakettle whistling as Paul ducked through the door of my solitary crib.

"Let me review one or two items, just to make sure we're skosh," I said and gathered the will in my hand.

Paul listened to me read the final revisions without comment and then without ceremony reached out for my pen.

"Show me where to make my mark."

I guided his signature at perhaps three or four places on the instrument, the original, first, and then its duplicate.

"There you go."

I took back my fountain pen. Paul leaned back in a chair threatening to collapse and fetched out his tobacco pouch.

"Got a pipe I can borrow, Johnny?"

I reached up to the rack he'd whittled for me ages earlier and pulled out a briar for myself and a clay pipe for Paul.

"Pretty sure this used to belong to Red Murphy." I handed it over.

Paul grunted confirmation and filled the bowl with leaf from his beaded pouch.

"Here," he said and put his talisman on my desk. "I want you to have it."

"You've given me plenty, Paul."

"I want you to have it."

"It's too personal."

"The better to remember me."

"As though there's a chance in hell I'd forget."

"Still." He shrugged, but did not press the issue.

I filled my bowl from the pouch and tamped it down. Then

I struck a match for both of us, and for a moment we lapsed into silence. Not a sound but the pleasant repercussion of smoke percolating through briar and clay.

It was around midafternoon at the camp, a near-mirror in climate and temperature to our first conversation about wills and testaments. As we smoked, the school's bell sounded, and within moments a gaggle of children spilled out and once again Paul turned to my window.

"Remember that time we watched 'em sledding, Johnny? Was a new snow, right on that slope over yonder."

"I do remember, yes."

Paul smiled.

"They've grown, haven't they? In just these few months."

"I 'spose they have."

"You know, I'd of give a lot to have a boy."

"I know you would."

"But you think I'd of been any good for him? A youngster needs his papa near to hand. Here I been gallivantin' all over."

"You'd have managed. Piotir managed for you."

"True enough." He sighed. "True enough."

We sat without a word for another interval. Just the two of us smoking. Then Paul heaved up from his chair, leaning at the waist so as not to take out my ceiling, and pointed the stem of his pipe toward the door.

"I'll be on the porch."

I said I'd join him soon as I got his paperwork secured.

Paul ducked outside and I slipped the original of his will into its own manila folder, followed that same routine with the duplicating copy, and then twirled the tumblers to open the safe in my office.

I couldn't have been more than three or four minutes in that task, and with the documents safely locked up, I left my small prefab to join Paul. I didn't see him at first, but the porch wraps around on two sides so I rounded the corner, and there was Red Murphy's pipe glowing on a porch swing I'd just put in that spring.

It's a lovers' swing, I guess you could say, a bench and back of red cedar built for two and hung by chains from a beam above. A stir of breeze fanned the embers still glowing in the pipe's clay bowl.

"*PAUL—?*"

I called out.

"*PAUL?!*"

I must have waited on that swing an hour before I could tolerate the possibility that he was gone for good. Clearly God is indifferent to an inkslinger's prayers; I did not see Paul that evening or any after.

In the years following, I've heard many larger-than-life tales involving Paul Bunyan or Babe. I can't validate any of those accounts and bearing in mind Paul's aversion to embellishment, I should probably discount them altogether.

But something deep inside human beings of any tribe needs legends to live along with the heroes and villains in them. We need Paul and Hel Helson and Swede Sturleson today for much the same reasons the Greeks needed Achilles and Hector and Agamemnon. These are the narratives that shape our lives and our dreams. Speaking of which—

I had a dream last night.

I found myself in a deep forest near a river under a bright and cloudless sky. There was a season's worth of logs boomed off in a dam on the river, and I could hear head waters gorging the sluices. As I watched, a log of white pine came barreling down a steep flume to crash on the pond below, and when that stick hit, it raised a spray of water that broke in bright sunlight to make a perfect rainbow.

Shimmering in the air in crescents from red to purple.

But I couldn't see a logger or river hog anywhere. That was impossible! There were thousands of sticks already boomed with thousands more set to slide down the chute. There had to be a camp nearby, a cutting crew, at least.

But then a tree swayed on a ridgeline above the reservoir, and I caught a glimpse of plaid as large as a ship's sail. There was Paul Bunyan striding along, taking a ridge at a time in boots big as a boat. Babe pulling a section of timber just behind. I tried to call out, but of course no sound would come.

You can't summon ghosts in dreams or legends.

I woke in my narrow cot and the dream faded, like a rainbow. Every now and then I open my floor safe and see the clay pipe and the beaded pouch. I take out the handwritten testament bequeathed by my friend and comrade, and I am reminded that Paul and his men do not need legends or tall tales to be remembered. A logger's life is magnificent and obdurate and stark.

There is no need to exaggerate.

...finis...

CPSIA information can be obtained
at www.ICGtesting.com
Printed in the USA
FSOW01n1751131115
13409FS